# MYSTERY OF THE BAMBOO BIRD

When a bamboo Garuda bird containing a sacred gold statue is stolen from Malee Wongsuwan at Starhurst School, she begs her friends, Louise and Jean Dana, to help recover the treasured possessions.

Despite a warning of possible danger, the Danas agree to take the case. Their efforts to apprehend the thief take the three girls across the United States and on to Malee's native country, Thailand. In Bangkok, the city of magnificent temples and picturesque canals, a trail of puzzling clues and a series of harrowing experiences await the young detectives.

This thrilling story of Louise and Jean's adventures in the Far East makes fascinating reading.

They were in imminent danger of being thrown off.

The *Dana Girls* Mystery Stories

# MYSTERY of the BAMBOO BIRD

## By Carolyn Keene

GROSSET & DUNLAP
A National General Company
*Publishers* *New York*

PUBLISHED SIMULTANEOUSLY IN CANADA
LIBRARY OF CONGRESS CATALOG CARD NUMBER: 73-815
ISBN: 0-448-09089-9

PRINTED IN THE UNITED STATES OF AMERICA

# CONTENTS

CHAPTER I

# The Missing Student

LOUISE DANA woke out of a sound sleep and blinked through slitted eyelids at the radium-dial clock beside her bed. Three A.M.! She was about to snuggle down again when she became aware of the smell of smoke.

Slim, dark-haired Louise instantly sat up in bed and sniffed. No doubt about it! There was a fire in Starhurst School.

She ran at once to the hall door, opened it, and stepped out into the long corridor of the dormitory, a wing of the three-story colonial building. The pungent odor of smoke came from the far end of the hall, where a stairway led down to the offices and classrooms located in the center section of the building.

Immediately Louise turned back into the room and called to her sister Jean, asleep on the other twin bed. At the same time she flicked the light switch. Nothing happened.

"Jean!" Louise cried out a second time. As her blond sister, sixteen and a year younger than she, sat up, Louise shouted, "Starhurst is on fire! We must warn everybody!"

Jean threw back the covers and jumped out of bed.

Quickly both girls pulled on heavy bathrobes and slid their feet into slippers.

"The lights are out!" Louise said. "Grab a flashlight!"

The sisters rushed into the hall. Wisps of smoke curled up the front stairway.

"I'll sound the fire alarm, but we'd better call all the girls, anyway," Louise suggested.

"I'll take the third floor." Jean dashed to a rear stairway of the old wooden building.

Louise ran to the fire-alarm box, broke the glass, and pulled the ring inside which automatically set off the warning gong. At the same time, it notified the Penfield fire and police departments.

The response from the sleepy students was not immediate, and Louise opened door after door, crying out, "Hurry! Get up! Put on your robe and slippers! Starhurst is on fire!"

The smell of smoke was now very pronounced and each girl quickly complied until Louise came to the room occupied by Lettie Briggs and Ina Mason.

"What's this? Some kind of joke?" Lettie complained. "The idea of having a fire drill at three o'clock in the morning. Well, *I'm* not going outside in this freezing cold weather!"

"You will unless you want to be burned up," Louise retorted. "Come out here and you can smell the smoke yourself."

"We'd better go," Ina spoke up fearfully. Sulkily her roommate agreed.

By this time Jean had aroused the students on the third floor, who came rushing down the back stairway pell-mell. All were alarmed, but thanks to the Danas' calm warning, they were not hysterical.

When the girls reached the second-floor landing, they saw the dignified headmistress, Mrs. Crandall, hurrying up the stairs. She spread her arms to stop them for a moment.

"There is no reason to be alarmed," the headmistress assured them. "The fire trucks are on their way. Just keep your heads—*do not run*—and no one will be hurt. I'll meet you in the garden. I want to check every room."

Without a word, the girls continued to the first floor and out into the garden. As the last girls came out, fire trucks and police squad cars roared into the grounds and came to a stop at the front of the burning building. The men focused huge floodlights on the scene.

The fire chief's car followed and in a few moments he was barking orders. Some of his men dragged a fire hose into the main entrance, others rushed to the rear of the building, and a third group waited to mount a ladder being swung upward from a truck to the second floor of the main section.

By this time the central part of the school building was a mass of flames. Many of the students began to cry and the Danas were close to tears. Mrs. Crandall appeared with her husband, mild-mannered Professor Crandall, and asked the girls to line up for roll call.

"Alice Andrews," she began.

"Here!"

By the time Mrs. Crandall had called the Danas' names, the sisters had studied the group of students. Suddenly they stared at each other, their faces white with fear. Every girl was there but one.

"Malee Wongsuwan is missing!" Jean gasped.

It was true. The lovely girl from Thailand, who was a new student at Starhurst and a close friend of the Danas, was not with the others. By some chance was she still in the building?

"We must find her!" Louise said.

"Maybe she was so terrified she hid in her closet," Jean suggested.

Together the sisters darted out of line and rushed up to Mrs. Crandall. They told her about Malee, and Jean added, "We'll go look in her closet and under the bed. The fire hasn't reached the dormitory wing yet."

"Be careful," the headmistress warned.

Louise and Jean dashed off, entered the building, and started up the rear stairway. When they

Louise and Jean ran toward the burning building
to rescue Malee.

reached the second floor, smoke was swirling toward them. A fireman barred their progress.

"You can't come up here! Get out!" he ordered.

"One of the girls is missing!" Louise cried. "We're afraid she panicked and may be hiding. Please look! Her room's up the hall just the other side of the linen closet."

"Okay."

As he left them, the man pulled a smoke mask over his face. Louise and Jean hurried down the stairs and rushed to a position beneath Malee's window. They waited anxiously and in a moment the fireman appeared at the window.

"Nobody in this room," he called down.

"Has her bed been slept in?" Louise asked.

"Yes," came the answer.

Louise had a sudden hunch that Malee might have run away. If so, she would have taken her most precious possession. Louise asked the fireman:

"Is there a large golden bamboo bird with red wings hanging over the bed?"

"A *what?*" he asked, puzzled.

Louise repeated her question. The man went back to look, then reported that there was no bamboo bird in the room.

Louise and Jean exchanged glances. "If Malee knew about the fire before we did, she would've warned the rest of us," Louise said. "What could have happened?"

Word was passed to the various firemen in the building and a thorough search was made for the missing student. Finally the chief came to tell Mrs. Crandall and the others that they were sure Malee Wongsuwan was not inside the school.

"Then where is she?" Lettie Briggs observed tartly. "I've always said there was something odd about that girl. And now I'm sure of it. And that bamboo bird of hers. What's so precious about it, anyhow?"

No one answered the unpleasant Lettie. She was a suspicious and complaining girl who never had a kind word for anybody.

Mrs. Crandall now ordered everyone to the gymnasium. This building stood apart from the main section of the school. The students, shivering in the early November air, were glad to hurry indoors.

A couple of the girls had become hysterical, crying out that they would lose everything. Others were unusually quiet, wondering if this would be the end of their beloved Starhurst. Among these were two of the Danas' best friends, Doris Harland and Evelyn Starr. Evelyn's ancestors had built Starhurst.

Louise and Jean continued to discuss Malee and her bamboo bird. The Thai girl had told them it was a replica, and the only one of its kind, of the sacred Garuda bird. Malee had once remarked that it would bring her good luck or bad luck, depending upon her actions. She had never explained exactly what she had meant.

Louise and Jean, still worried about Malee, entered the gymnasium, where they found hot cocoa and buns. Despite all the excitement, Mrs. Crandall had ordered the food from the all-night lunch counter in Penfield.

The girls finished eating, then talked about the school disaster. At five o'clock the fire chief strode in and declared that the fire was out.

"It will be perfectly safe for some of you young ladies to return to your rooms," he said. "We have roped off the damaged area. But please use the rear stairway and don't try going beyond the barrier."

Mrs. Crandall announced that school would be suspended for two months. She said that the students might leave the gymnasium now if they wished, but were to report back there at seven o'clock for further instructions and at that time were to telephone their parents or guardians that they would be home.

"I'd hate to leave here without knowing whether or not Malee is safe," Louise whispered to Jean.

The Danas were delighted to discover that their study and bedroom had not been damaged, but everything reeked with the pungent odor of smoke.

Jean gave a wry smile. "I hate the idea of putting on a smoky skirt and sweater," she said.

Louise was thoughtful. "Before we dress, let's

take a look in Malee's room and see if we can find out anything. Maybe she packed and left before the fire."

The sisters hurried up the hall and thoroughly investigated the Thai girl's bedroom. Finally Louise remarked, "It looks as though nothing is missing except her bathrobe and slippers. If I'm right, that means she did leave here at the time of the fire or before it."

"But why?" Jean asked, staring out the window.

Before Louise could even guess at an answer, the Danas heard loud complaints from Lettie Briggs, whose room was in the roped-off section. She flatly declared that she was going to it despite the fire chief's orders.

"Don't be silly," Jean said, coming into the hall with Louise. "It must be dangerous, or the chief wouldn't have told us to stay away."

Lettie threw her head back haughtily. "Oh, don't be childish. I guess I know danger when I see it."

Fortunately for the obstinate girl, Mrs. Crandall appeared and refused to allow Lettie to enter the roped-off section. To add to the girl's discomfiture, the headmistress suggested that since Louise Dana wore the same size as Lettie, she would no doubt be glad to lend her some clothes.

"Help yourself," Louise said with a smile.

Lettie, who had very expensive and exclusive clothes, did not look too pleased with the plan, but she finally followed the sisters to their room. She helped herself to the lingerie which Louise saved for party week ends, a lovely red woolen dress, a new pair of leather shoes, and a sports coat.

Louise said nothing, but bit her lip a couple of times in exasperation. She knew that Lettie deliberately had chosen some of her best things, and besides, probably would never make any attempt to return the clothes.

Jean and Louise spent the next two hours dressing and packing. At seven o'clock they carried their bags to the first floor, then went to the gymnasium.

"Let's phone Aunt Harriet now," Louise said.

Miss Harriet Dana and her brother Ned, captain of the Atlantic ocean liner *Balaska*, lived together in Oak Falls. They were the guardians of the orphaned sisters, whose parents had died several years ago.

"Starhurst burned!" the girls' startled aunt exclaimed when she heard the news. "Oh, thank goodness no one was hurt. Please give Mrs. Crandall my sympathy. This is dreadful. But I will be glad to have you girls home for the next two months."

Aunt Harriet suggested that they come by train. She would meet them with the car. "And, if you like, bring one of your friends with you," she added before hanging up.

Breakfast was served in the gymnasium and Mrs. Crandall gave out final instructions, including partial homework assignments which had been prepared quickly by various teachers to whom Mrs. Crandall had talked.

"You'll receive more assignments by mail," she added. "The school will pay for any necessary tutoring."

Louise and Jean told her what train they planned to take and Mrs. Crandall said a taxi would be waiting to take them to the Penfield station. The girls delivered Aunt Harriet's message, and again expressed their own sorrow at the fire.

"Let's go back to our room and pick up the books we'll need," Louise suggested to her sister.

The two girls had gone barely a hundred feet across the lawn when they saw a weary, bedraggled figure in bathrobe and slippers coming across a field near the tennis courts.

"It's Malee!" Jean exclaimed, and she and Louise began to run at top speed toward her.

CHAPTER II

# Mysterious Thief

"LOUISE! Jean!" cried Malee Wongsuwan as she fell into the sisters' arms, exhausted. But a second later she saw the ruined school building and cried, wide-eyed, "What—what happened here?"

The Danas stared at the Thai girl in amazement. Finally Jean asked, "You mean you didn't know there was a fire at Starhurst?"

"No, oh no!" Malee replied, shocked. Her beautiful brown eyes filled with tears and her round olive-skinned face looked worried. "This is the second bit of bad luck," she murmured.

"Second?" Louise repeated. "What do you mean, Malee? And are *you* all right? We've been frantic about you."

As Louise and Jean waited expectantly for the answer, they wondered if there could be a mystery connected with her temporary disappearance. The sisters loved solving mysteries and had already encountered several situations in which, fortunately, they had been able to help various people solve perplexing problems.

The Danas' first real case had started right in their home town, Oak Falls, and was called *Mystery of the Stone Tiger*. Recently they had visited the island of Chincoteague, Virginia, to solve the mystery of *The Haunted Lagoon*.

"You must have thought I ran away to escape the fire," Malee said wearily. "No, it was not that. I suddenly awoke to see a man climbing out of the window with my precious bamboo Garuda bird."

"A thief!" Jean exclaimed.

Malee nodded. "I was very frightened, but I called to him, 'Stop! Bring back my bird!' To my surprise he answered me in Thai, and I realized I had called to him in Thai."

As Malee paused, Jean said impatiently, "What did he say?"

"He was very rude," Malee replied. "The man called back, 'You will never find this bird. It is going to New York to be sold. And do not send the police after me or you will be harmed!' "

"How dreadful!" Louise cried out.

She asked if Malee had been able to get a good look at the intruder. The girl shook her head and answered, "He had a big scarf over his head and shoulders. It hid his face, and anyway, it was still dark—only half after two o'clock."

Malee said she had quickly put on her bathrobe and slippers and climbed out the window to try to make the man give back the bird. "As you know, my window is over the porte-cochere, so I had no trouble climbing down."

"Then what happened?" Louise asked.

"The thief ran very fast. I had a hard time keeping him in sight, but I might have caught up to him if he had not gone into the woods over there."

Malee pointed to a distant hillside forest. "It was so dark in the woods I finally had to give up. But when I tried to find my way back to Starhurst I realized I was lost. I walked in circles for hours and hours until I found the right direction. I must have been so far away I didn't even see the fire."

"You poor girl!" Louise said sympathetically, and offered to accompany Malee to her room. "Jean, will you go tell Mrs. Crandall that Malee is back?"

Jean hurried off, but returned in a few minutes to say that as soon as Malee was dressed, she was to see Mrs. Crandall.

When the three girls arrived at the headmistress' apartment, which was on the first floor of the unburned section, Mrs. Crandall asked for a complete recount of Malee's adventure. She frowned several times, then said, "You've had a trying experience indeed, my dear. This is a most serious matter. Your bamboo bird must be of great value for a person to go to such lengths to steal it."

"It is," Malee answered.

"Have you any idea who the thief might be?" the headmistress asked.

"No, Mrs. Crandall."

"Just what do you estimate the bird to be worth?" the headmistress inquired.

Malee hung her head and did not answer at once. Then, looking up and smiling faintly, she said, "A great deal of money. But I was thinking of the sentimental side, and what is of great value to one from my country might not be of value to anyone in yours."

Suddenly Malee began to sway and the Danas feared she would faint. At once Mrs. Crandall became solicitous. "Why, you haven't had breakfast," she said. "I'll have something brought here immediately from the gymnasium."

"I will be all right to walk there," the Thai girl insisted. "But I am very hungry."

The Danas went with her. Upon entering the gymnasium and seeing that the other girls were eager to ask questions about her disappearance, Malee begged Louise and Jean to make excuses for her.

"I sure will," Jean said stanchly.

To each student who approached she said, "No questions until Malee has had breakfast."

The Danas insisted that their friend sit down, and brought her fruit juice, milk, and toast.

"I feel much better now," Malee announced when she finished eating.

Near the trio a large group of girls were making plans for the next two months. Invitations for visits flew back and forth. The chattering ceased when the headmistress entered and clapped her hands for attention.

"There are several newspaper photographers and reporters on the grounds," Mrs. Crandall said. "It has come to my attention that some of you have been talking to them about the fire. Please do not do so. Any further information will be given out by me or the police. I will also get in touch with the insurance company. If any of you girls have claims, will you please write me about them from your homes."

Mrs. Crandall turned and left the building. She had been gone less than five minutes when two young men came in. They looked around at the students.

Finally spotting Malee Wongsuwan, they came toward her. Quickly one of them held up a camera. But before he could snap a picture, Jean jumped in front of the girl. She turned her back to the photographer just as the flash bulb went off.

"Hey, what's the big idea?" the young man demanded angrily.

Jean turned. "You have no right to take pictures here without permission," she said.

The man's companion started to laugh. "Permission?" he repeated. "With a big story like a missing golden bamboo bird?"

Louise, Jean, and Malee stared coldly at the reporter. But he was not dismayed. Coming forward and planting himself directly in front of Malee, he said, "Now listen, beautiful, don't think your story isn't known. Surely you don't want the paper to print anything that's untrue. How about giving me an exclusive?"

Malee looked appealingly toward the Danas. Louise answered the question. "Any information will have to come from Mrs. Crandall. But there's one thing I'd like to know. Where did you get the story about a missing bamboo bird?"

The reporter and the photographer lifted their eyebrows, then admitted it was a fireman who had told them. "But you're not the one to ask questions," the reporter said. "I am. Now, what about telling me the truth?"

"We'll find Mrs. Crandall for you," Louise offered, gritting her teeth.

The young men, seeing that an interview with Malee was hopeless, said they would locate the headmistress themselves. They left the gymnasium. Malee looked worried, but Jean merely grinned.

"Don't think any more about it, Malee," she advised. "Mrs. Crandall won't tell those men one thing."

Louise, changing the subject abruptly, said, "Malee, Jean and I have a surprise for you. We were talking to our Aunt Harriet on the phone a while ago. We're inviting you to spend the next two months with us."

Malee's face broke into a happy smile and she grasped each sister by the hand. "Oh, you are such darling friends," she said. "But I could not impose on you for that long a time. Anyway," she added, "Mrs. Crandall is responsible for me during the school term."

At once the Danas assured Malee that Mrs. Crandall would agree to the arrangement. "Let's go and ask her right now," Jean proposed.

The three girls went to Mrs. Crandall's apartment and readily obtained permission for Malee to accompany the sisters to their home in Oak Falls. If she did not wish to spend the entire time there, the headmistress told Malee that she could come back to the school and stay with her.

"In the meantime, I think that your whereabouts should remain a secret, Malee," the headmistress advised. "I am really very much concerned that the thief threatened you. This could mean that you may be in danger. You must take every precaution. I have a suggestion to offer. If anyone tries to get in touch with you, either in person or by telephone, it would be wise to have the person identify himself to the Danas. Then they can decide whether it is all right for you to talk to the caller."

Malee agreed to the plan and the Danas went to help her pack. As they worked, the subject of the bamboo bird came up again. Suddenly Louise said, "I wonder if that thief, either on purpose or accidentally, set Starhurst on fire."

Malee's eyes grew round as saucers. "If it *was* done deliberately, what a wicked thing to do!" She walked to the hall door and closed it, then came up to the Danas and in a whisper confided, "I am going to tell you a secret. There *is* something very valuable inside the bamboo bird and I believe the thief knew that."

"Do you want to tell us what it is?" Louise asked.

"Yes, I do," Malee answered. "But I would prefer that you do not tell anyone else at Starhurst. As you know, I follow a different religion from you and the other students here. You would understand, but I am afraid some of the others might not. I am a Buddhist. Inside the bird was a gold statue of our great religious teacher Buddha. His garments are outlined in star sapphires, rubies, and zircons."

Louise and Jean gasped in amazement.

Malee went on, "When it was decided that I would spend this year at Starhurst, my father had the statue made for me of gold from the mine he owns. When I was alone in my room, I would take the statue out of the bird and sit in contemplation. You know, we Buddhists try to receive enlightenment by gazing at the great leader's face, and then practice tolerance in our daily lives."

"It is a very beautiful religion," Louise observed.

"I presume the Buddha statue was hidden inside the bird not only for safekeeping, but for privacy, as well."

Malee nodded and smiled. "I am so glad you understand. I was sure you would."

"I'm terribly sorry the bird and statue were taken," said Jean. "Don't you think you should notify the police?"

"I am afraid it would do no good," Malee replied. "The thief is far away by this time. But I will ask Mrs. Crandall to tell the police."

"Do you think," Jean asked, "that the thief may remove the gems and even break up the gold and sell everything?"

"I hope not," Malee replied sadly. "No, I believe he has other plans—for the statue, at least." Wistfully she added, "It would make me so happy to find my bird and its precious contents."

Louise asked, "Do you suppose the thief knows you?"

"I have no idea," the girl answered. "But he must have known where my room is." She sighed. "But I feel so lonesome without my beautiful Garuda bird and comforting Buddha."

Jean glanced at her watch and reminded the others that it was almost time to leave for the station. Malee had walked over to her desk and now absently picked up an opened letter.

Suddenly her relaxed mood changed to one of tenseness. Malee turned to the girls and startled them by saying she could not go with them to Oak Falls after all. Evidently the letter had reminded her of something which made her change her mind!

"Why not?" Jean asked, astounded.

"I must leave at once for Bangkok," Malee replied. "I have a feeling that it is imperative!"

The Danas looked at her speechlessly. The girl from Thailand unexpectedly came up to the two sisters and gave each of them a hug. They could see that she was stoically fighting back tears.

"Girls," she said, in a voice full of emotion, "you are the dearest friends I have ever had. I need your help very much. I must go to my home in Bangkok immediately. Could you possibly come with me?"

## CHAPTER III

# Preparations for Bangkok

"BANGKOK!" Jean cried out. "Oh, I wish we *could* go, but of course that would be impossible."

"We could never afford it," Louise added.

Malee smiled and said, "Not long ago I had a letter from my father. He wrote, 'When you come home next summer, would you not like to bring a friend or two as your guests? I shall be delighted to bear all the expense of such a trip.' Mrs. Crandall is giving us an enforced vacation, and I can invite you to be my guests, all the way from Starhurst to Bangkok and back."

Louise and Jean were almost speechless with surprise. In their various talks with Malee she had described her country as if it were a fascinating fairyland. And now here was an opportunity actually to see it themselves.

Before the Danas had a chance to reply, Malee begged, "Please come! I need you to help solve the mystery of my stolen bamboo bird and I somehow feel you will find the answer to this puzzle in Bangkok. And there is another matter which I cannot tell you about yet. I must first consult my family. But I believe the two mysteries are linked. If you come, I am sure you will give all the Wongsuwans peace of mind. I consider you great detectives."

Impulsively Jean gave Malee an affectionate squeeze. "You're amazing and wonderful and—and I just can't thank you enough."

"I feel the same way," Louise added. "But perhaps you are putting too much faith in us and our abilities as amateur sleuths."

"I have a strong feeling that you will solve one and perhaps two mysteries," Malee said with determination. "Also, I believe you cannot do it unless you come to Bangkok."

The sisters laughed and Jean said, "Since you put it that way, how can we refuse?"

"But we must ask Aunt Harriet and Uncle Ned," Louise reminded Jean and Malee. "And besides, if we do go, we'll have to get our summer clothes from Oak Falls."

Malee suddenly danced with joy. "In that case, I will accompany you to your home. I will convince your good aunt and uncle of the importance of your mission."

Quickly the girls put on coats and hats, and grabbed books and assignments. With their luggage loaded into the cab, they drove to the railroad station. The platform was crowded with Starhurst students and Penfield residents.

The three girls made their way through the huge crowd to get near the tracks. As they stood waiting for the train, many eyes were turned in the direction of the beautiful, black-haired girl from Thailand.

"I wish people would not stare at me," Malee remarked plaintively. "It seems as if *everyone* must know about the bamboo bird."

"Oh, I'm sure that the news couldn't have reached all these people so quickly," Louise said gently.

Malee's eyes were roving over the crowd. Suddenly she grasped Louise's arm. "That woman in the red hat. Do you know who she is?" she asked.

Both Louise and Jean said they had never seen the woman and inquired why Malee wanted to know.

"She's wearing a Thai scarf—a beautiful one with our sacred Garuda bird embroidered on it in gold. I wonder where she got it."

"Let's ask her," Jean proposed, and walked over to the woman. Louise and Malee followed.

"I hope you don't mind my asking," Jean said to her, "but we were wondering where you got your beautiful scarf."

"A friend brought it to me from Bangkok," the woman replied, then, looking straight at Malee, she added, "You could be a Thai yourself."

Malee admitted that she was. Instantly the woman said, "Oh, you must be the Thai girl who is a student at Starhurst. My friend told me about you."

Malee, startled, asked who the friend was. She was told that his name was Swad Holden.

"I never heard of him," said Malee. "I wonder how he knew about me."

The woman, who now introduced herself as Mrs. Randolph from Penfield, explained that Swad Holden's mother was a Thai. "His father was English," she added.

Louise and Jean glanced at each other, and Louise said, "How interesting! Where does Mr. Holden live?"

Mrs. Randolph laughed. "To tell you the truth, he has no real home—travels all the time. My husband and I met him on a ship last year when we were returning from Europe. The ship's marvelous. It's the *Balaska*. Did you ever hear of it?"

"Why, yes," replied Jean. But before she could reveal that Uncle Ned was the vessel's captain, Louise threw her a warning glance.

Immediately Jean realized why. From what Mrs. Randolph had told them so far, there might be a link between Swad Holden and the missing bamboo bird. After all, he was part Thai, he knew of Malee, and was familiar with the vicinity of Penfield.

Louise now asked Mrs. Randolph, "When did you last see Mr. Holden?"

"He came to our home just last evening," the woman replied. "Dropped in out of a clear sky. He stayed scandalously late, and my husband was angry about it." Mrs. Randolph giggled. "My husband likes to talk, but when Swad's around, he can't get a word in edgewise."

Louise's and Jean's pulses were racing. This might be the best clue yet to the thief of the bamboo bird! Swad Holden had been in town the evening before the Starhurst fire! He may even have had time to make inquiries and locate Malee's room.

Her brain working rapidly, Louise said, "Your scarf is so beautiful, Mrs. Randolph. Have you any idea if I could get one through Mr. Holden?"

"I'm sure he'd get one for you," the woman responded, "but I can't tell you where to find him. Swad didn't say where he was heading next."

Just then the girls heard the train coming. When it stopped, there was a mad scramble to get aboard. Mrs. Randolph stepped up to the platform just ahead of Malee and the Danas, hurried into a coach, and saved two facing seats for the four of them. "I enjoy talking to you girls," she said, "I hope you don't mind."

Louise and Jean not only did not mind, but thought perhaps they could find out more about Swad Holden! As the train roared along, Mrs. Randolph was very talkative, telling about her travels. Cleverly Louise switched the conversation back to the *Balaska* and Mr. Holden.

"He's handsome," Mrs. Randolph bubbled. "I do hope you meet him sometime. He's stocky and has eyes that can look right through you. His thick, dark hair is neatly styled. Swad is one of the best-groomed men I've ever met."

The Danas could clearly visualize him. Their interest led Mrs. Randolph into telling them several other things about the man: that he was about five feet nine inches tall, usually wore English-style clothes, and spoke with a combination English and American accent.

"I'm sure I'll recognize him if I meet him," Jean said with a giggle.

Mrs. Randolph bade the trio good-by at the next station and left the train. As the girls went on to Oak Falls, Louise told Malee of her suspicions regarding Swad Holden.

"You *are* fine detectives," Malee remarked.

Soon the train reached Oak Falls. As the Danas hurried down the steps to the platform, they saw not only their Aunt Harriet, but, to their delight, their Uncle Ned as well.

"My hearties!" the robust, seafaring man said with an expansive smile. He scooped both his nieces up off the ground and gave them affectionate embraces.

The sisters kissed their aunt, then introduced Malee. It was evident from the expressions of the two older Danas that they were charmed by the girl from Thailand.

"We're so pleased to have you visit us, Malee," said Aunt Harriet. Then, to her nieces, she announced, "Surprise! We have a new station wagon!"

"How wonderful!" the two girls exclaimed.

Beaming, Uncle Ned led the way to the sleek car.

"It is most attractive," Malee murmured. The luggage was put into the back and everyone climbed in. As they drove home, Louise asked her uncle if he remembered a passenger he had carried on his ship the year before by the name of Swad Holden.

"Indeed I do," the sea captain replied. "Quite a fellow, Holden. Could speak several languages. Great entertainer, too. He loved to play character parts in the little skits passengers put on. By the way, how do you know about him?"

"We think he may be a thief!" Jean blurted out.

"A thief!" Aunt Harriet repeated. "What did he steal?"

Briefly the three girls related the story of the missing golden bamboo Garuda. Uncle Ned frowned, and remarked that he could understand why his nieces felt suspicious of Holden.

"Of course you never can tell about people," he remarked. "But on board the *Balaska* I never heard anything unfavorable about him."

Aunt Harriet spoke up. "It seems very odd that the man has no permanent address."

"That's true," her brother agreed. "Tell you what. When I get back to the *Balaska*, I'll look up the records at the steamship office and let you girls know what address Holden gave at the time he booked passage."

It was not until late afternoon that Malee broached the subject of Louise and Jean accompanying her to Bangkok. When she did, Aunt Harriet and Uncle Ned were amazed by the invitation. At first they both felt that the Danas would be far too indebted to the Wongsuwans.

"But I need Louise and Jean very much to help me solve not only one, but two mysteries," Malee said pleadingly. "My father can well afford to pay for the trip, and it would mean so much to my entire family."

Aunt Harriet did not think it safe for the girls to travel alone, particularly in view of the fact that Malee might be in danger.

But Captain Dana boomed out, "I think I have the answer. Harriet, why don't you go with the girls? I'll be happy to pay your fare."

Before their aunt had a chance to object, her nieces ran to Uncle Ned and threw their arms about his neck. "You're a dear, a perfect dear!" Jean exclaimed. "Then it's all settled."

It took a little more persuasion before Aunt Harriet was thoroughly convinced that the trip was feasible, but finally she consented.

"Oh, thank you, thank you so very much," said

Malee. "I have a cousin in the Thai Embassy in Washington. May I use your telephone to call him? I will ask him to get in touch with my parents and also make plane reservations for all of us as soon as possible."

As Louise walked to the telephone with Malee, she reminded her of Mrs. Crandall's advice. "Tell your cousin when he phones here to ask for one of us Danas and identify himself."

Malee nodded and put in the call to her cousin, who said he would be happy to undertake the assignment.

"One thing he said to ask you was whether the three of you had been vaccinated recently," Malee told them.

Jean giggled. "You name it and we've had it," she said. "Because of our travels to various countries, Louise and Aunt Harriet and I have had smallpox, typhoid, cholera, and yellow fever inoculations."

It was Malee's turn to laugh. "That's more than I've had. I'm happy that Thailand and the United States require only smallpox vaccinations of each other."

"Then we're all set," Louise spoke up. "Malee, we'd like to show off our little town. Would you care to drive around Oak Falls?"

"I should love to," their guest replied. "Everything looks so different from my city. We have many canals." Malee then asked the two sisters excitedly, "Do you think your uncle would let me drive the station wagon? I have an international license, but I have not been behind the wheel of a car since I left Bangkok."

"I'll ask him," Louise offered.

Uncle Ned had no objection and suggested certain points of interest in the town for the Danas to show Malee. He backed the car from the driveway to the street. Malee slid in behind the wheel and Louise and Jean sat in the front seat with her. She waved good-by to Captain Dana and started down the street. Almost at once Malee crossed to the left side and speeded up the car.

"Goodness! What's she doing?" Louise gasped to herself. She opened her mouth to protest, but at this moment Jean directed, "Left here, Malee."

The girl from Thailand turned very abruptly, still on the wrong side of the street. As she rounded the corner, the Danas were horrified to see a car coming directly toward them.

"Move over!" Jean cried out.

But Malee seemed frozen to the wheel. She jammed on the brake, but did not swerve.

The other car was almost upon them when Louise, who was seated in the middle, grabbed the wheel. Could she possibly get out of the way in time?

CHAPTER IV

# Danger

THE Dana station wagon was jerked from the path of the oncoming car just in the nick of time. Louise jammed on the brake and stopped.

"Oh, what a dreadful thing I did!" Malee cried. "In my country we drive on the left-hand side of the road. I forgot that here it is the opposite. But that is no excuse. Please forgive me, Louise—Jean."

Before the Danas could reply, the driver of the other car stormed across the street and shook his fist at Malee.

"What are you trying to do, you crazy driver?" he yelled. "Smash us all up?"

Malee, who was now trembling, could only murmur, "I am sorry—dreadfully sorry."

"Sorry!" the man continued. "Why, we might all have landed in the hospital!"

"But we didn't," Louise spoke up calmly. "My friend has apologized. What more can she do? You are not hurt."

"No, but my nerves are shattered." He stared at Malee, then added unkindly, "You're a foreigner, aren't you? What business have you got driving here in Oak Falls?"

Still Malee did not reply. She was too stunned, both by the near accident and the man's blustering manner. But Jean asked the stranger who he was.

"I'm Ray Smith and I live on the next street. Who are you?"

Jean told him and at once the man's manner softened. "You're the nieces of Captain Dana?" he asked. "I know him well. Well, let's forget the whole thing. But in the future, be careful, young lady," he cautioned Malee.

Without another word, he walked back to his own car, jumped in, and drove off.

"Louise, will you please take the wheel?" Malee requested. "And if you do not mind, I would like to go back to your house."

"Of course."

When the girls returned to the Dana residence they did not mention the unpleasant incident to Aunt Harriet and Uncle Ned. Instead, Louise and Jean said they were tired and had decided to postpone the sightseeing drive. Everyone went to bed early and by morning Malee was her usual cheerful self.

While the family was eating breakfast, the telephone rang. Aunt Harriet answered and said that the call was for Malee. "It's a woman," she added.

Malee and the Dana girls looked concerned. They had forgotten to tell Aunt Harriet of the plan to relay all of Malee's calls through the Danas.

"Oh, dear!" Malee said worriedly. "What shall I do?"

"Suppose you just listen to what the woman has to say," Jean suggested. "I'll get on the upstairs extension and say hello. If there's any trouble, I'll take over on the conversation."

Malee agreed. In a minute Jean picked up the phone and said, "Hello."

In a somewhat muffled voice, the stranger replied, "Miss Wongsuwan, I'm calling to tell you that I learned your present address. I have your bamboo bird. Don't ask me how I got it. If you want it back, this is what you're to do. Put one hundred dollars in an envelope, take it to the little park opposite the firehouse in Oak Falls, and put it under some leaves by the large oak tree."

There was a pause. Finally the strange woman went on, "Under that same pile of leaves you will find instructions as to where the bird is."

Again there was complete silence on the Danas' end of the line. The speaker, apparently impatient, said, "Well, are you going to do it?"

Malee remained still, but suddenly Jean broke into an uproarious laugh. "Okay, Lettie Briggs," she said. "What made you think we'd fall for such a hoax?"

There was a snort on the other end of the line. Then the voice, which to Jean obviously had been disguised, now burst out in Lettie's familiar nasal tone, "Oh, burn up!" The receiver was slammed down.

Malee and Jean hung up, then met on the first floor. The girl from Thailand gazed at her friend in amazement. "How did you guess it was Lettie?"

Jean replied that if Malee had known Lettie as long as the Danas had, she would have detected the joke herself.

"Well," Malee sighed in relief, "I am thankful it was only a joke."

An hour later the telephone rang again. Miss Dana called Malee once more, telling her that her cousin at the Embassy in Washington was phoning. After a few minutes' conversation, Malee returned, a pleased smile on her face.

"My cousin says he has cabled my parents and they answered to say they are looking forward to your visit," she reported. "He has our plane reservations and we can pick them up at the Mission of Thailand office in New York."

"Do we go all the way by air?" Louise inquired.

"Yes. We fly from New York to San Francisco," Malee replied, "then to Honolulu, Tokyo, and on to Bangkok. When you arrive there, you will be halfway around the world!"

"It's absolutely thrilling!" Jean stated.

"Just think," Louise said, "at last we Danas are going to see all the beautiful sights and places you have told us about."

"I can't believe it!" Jean exclaimed. "Let's get our plans settled right away."

Malee asked Captain Dana to make reservations for the travelers from Oak Falls to New York. He agreed, and added that he thought they should go by plane. "I'll fly with you to New York," he said. "I'd like to have you see the *Balaska*, Malee, and I have some work to attend to before the ship sails."

"You mean find out about Swad Holden?" Jean asked eagerly.

The captain laughed heartily. "Yes, lass, and some work of my own, too." He turned to Malee. "You see, my nieces are right on the job. I venture to say they'll solve your mysteries for you long before it's time to return from Bangkok."

"Oh, I hope you are right," Malee said.

"We'd better pack now. Tell us exactly what to take," Jean urged Malee.

Malee suggested that they take both heavy and light clothes. "It will be warm in Honolulu and Bangkok, but chilly in San Francisco and Tokyo," Malee explained.

It took most of the day for the Danas to bring out summer clothes and look them over. Having traveled by air before, they knew the rules about how much baggage they could take without paying for excess weight. Sports attire and dresses were chosen, then all but the favorites were eliminated.

Finally Jean heaved a sigh. "I've packed and unpacked my bag four times," she declared. "And still I can't get the lid down."

Aunt Harriet smiled wisely. "Perhaps the trouble is too many shoes," she said. "How about only one extra pair of walking shoes and one for dress-up occasions?"

Jean pulled out a few pairs of shoes. This time the lid went down and when her suitcase was weighed it was three pounds under the limit.

That evening after dinner Aunt Harriet and Uncle Ned went out to visit some old friends. Left alone, Louise, Jean, and Malee drew up chairs around a roaring fire in the living room. They began to talk about the stolen bamboo bird.

Louise asked, "Malee, yesterday you told Jean and me that you wanted us to help you on two mysteries. You mentioned consulting your parents about the second one. Is this still true or would you like to tell us about it now?"

Malee did not reply for some time. She sat staring into the flames of the crackling wood. Louise and Jean looked at each other. Was their friend "in contemplation," asking for guidance in forming her answer to them?

Finally Malee looked up and said, "Louise and Jean, before I tell you what the second mystery is, I must find out certain things from my parents. And now I may be in danger because Mrs. Crandall told the police about my stolen bamboo bird—after that thief warned me not to—oh, dear, it is very selfish of me to expect you to run such a risk for a Wongsuwan."

Louise and Jean were amazed by this turn of events, but the possibility of danger had never swayed them from helping a friend. Before they could make any comment, however, Malee looked straight at the Dana sisters and said:

"Are you sure you still want to help me solve my mysteries?"

CHAPTER V

# Successful Sleuthing

LOUISE and Jean sympathized with Malee who seemed so worried, yet was thoughtful enough not to want them to get involved in any danger on her account.

Louise put an arm around the distressed girl. "Jean and I wouldn't desert you now for anything. We'd like to help protect you and solve the mysteries."

Jean chuckled. "Aren't we on the trail of the man we think was responsible for nearly burning up our dear old Starhurst? I'd certainly like to find him!"

Malee smiled. "You're such darlings," she said. "I am really very happy that you want to go with me but please be careful. I would not want anything to happen to you." After a pause she added, "Please forgive me for not telling you about the second mystery. Let's wait until we get to Bangkok. In the meantime, I want you girls to have a pleasant trip."

Out of deference to her request, the Danas said no more about Malee's secret, but they still wondered about it. The girls slept soundly and by morning were eager to start their exciting journey. A taxi took the group to the airport outside Oak Falls and they climbed aboard the plane for New York.

The flight was smooth and uneventful. As they neared the great city, Malee told the girls she had never been to New York and was fascinated with the thought of seeing its famous skyscrapers.

"I have always loved the idea of your Statue of Liberty," the girl from Thailand remarked. "It is so symbolic. I am glad that the people of my country too are free to come and go and do as they wish. How dreadful it must be to live in a place where this is not true!"

After disembarking at La Guardia Airport, Malee and the Danas took the airline's limousine in to the city terminal, then taxied to the dock where the *Balaska* was moored.

"Isn't she a beautiful ship?" Jean said enthusiastically.

"Oh, yes," Malee murmured.

Captain Dana said he would accompany his nieces to the steamship office to find out about Swad Holden. In the meantime, he suggested that

Aunt Harriet take Malee on a tour of the *Balaska* and scribbled out a visitors' pass for them.

"We'll meet you on board in about twenty minutes," the captain told his sister.

At the steamship office the Danas were told that Swad Holden had used a passport from England and had given a London hotel as his address. Captain Dana thanked the clerk and went aboard the *Balaska* with his nieces.

"Uncle Ned," said Louise, "would the steward who took care of Mr. Holden's cabin be working here now?"

"Yes. Would you like to talk to him?"

Louise nodded. "I thought maybe he could tell us something more about Mr. Holden."

Captain Dana took his nieces to the promenade deck where Holden had had a private cabin. He introduced them to Steward Tom Moore, then left them, saying, "I'll see you later, girls."

"I remember you young ladies well," Moore remarked. "You went to Europe with us, and became involved in some mystery."

"We're trying to solve another mystery," Louise told him. "We'd like to find out something about a passenger named Swad Holden."

"A stocky man with thick black hair?"

"That fits his description," Louise replied.

"Well, if you're asking whether I liked him or not, the answer is no. That man made a lot of trouble for me. Several times I nearly reported him to your uncle, but I kept still."

"What did he do?" Jean asked eagerly.

"Well, it was those fancy cigarettes of his. He smoked a high-priced English brand—Weathervane. Holden had a bad habit of lighting one, taking a few puffs, and then tossing it away. He never put it out and didn't seem to care where the cigarette landed."

"How dreadful!" Louise exclaimed. "He could easily start a fire with such carelessness."

The Danas looked at each other. Clues were pointing more and more to Swad Holden as the suspect who had entered Starhurst School! He had probably discarded a lighted cigarette, then had gone upstairs to steal the bamboo bird.

"You're right, Miss Louise," Tom Moore agreed. "Most every day on that trip I put out a smoldering cigarette which Mr. Holden had carelessly dropped on the carpet in his cabin. I got in the habit of checking his room the minute he left it."

The sisters talked a short while longer with the steward but learned nothing else of value, so they thanked him and said good-by. They met Aunt Harriet and Malee at the grand stairway and told them of their conversation with the steward.

"That sounds like rather damaging evidence," Aunt Harriet remarked. Then she said to Malee, "You haven't told the police everything about the theft. Don't you think you should?"

"Not yet, please," Malee requested earnestly. "It is possible that the thief was sent here by someone in my country to steal the bamboo bird with the gold Buddha in it. I must find out certain things in order to avoid any unpleasant family publicity."

The Danas hoped Malee would elaborate on this statement, but she said no more.

"Very well," Aunt Harriet replied. "But my advice is not to wait too long."

After Aunt Harriet and the three girls had said good-by to Captain Dana, they hailed a taxi and drove to the building in which the Thai Embassy had its New York office. Malee and the Danas identified themselves to a clerk who gave them their books of tickets.

"When you reach San Francisco," the clerk suggested, "check your reservations with the airline office there and do the same at the other airports where you stop."

As they left the office, Malee said she would like to go sightseeing. Aunt Harriet suggested they check in at their hotel first, so they drove back uptown. After getting settled, Aunt Harriet said, "Suppose you girls see the town by yourselves? I'd like to do a little shopping here before we take off tomorrow."

Her nieces agreed. They linked arms with Malee and went out to the street.

"Where shall we go first?" Malee asked, her eyes sparkling with excitement.

"I'd like to combine sightseeing with sleuthing," Jean spoke up.

"Good. How can we do that?" Malee asked.

"Maybe the man who stole the bamboo bird did bring it to New York to sell," Jean said. "Why don't we go to some of the better jewelry stores and make inquiries?"

"That's a wonderful idea," Louise agreed.

The Danas knew the names of several prominent jewelry shops, some of which were on Fifth Avenue. Thinking that Malee would be interested in seeing this famous thoroughfare, Louise hailed a taxi and instructed the driver to take them to Central Park. There the girls hopped out to begin their walk down the avenue.

As Louise had expected, Malee was charmed by the lovely park, the beautiful hotels, the modern office buildings, and the attractive department stores with their elaborate window displays.

At the first two jewelry shops where the girls stopped, they were told that no gold-covered bamboo bird had been brought in and offered for sale. This news brought a look of sadness to Malee's face.

"I'm afraid this is turning into a wild-goose chase," Jean was saying as they approached a third jewelry store. "But cheer up, we have several more—" She stopped speaking suddenly and cried out, "Look, Malee! There's your missing bamboo bird!"

“There’s your missing bird!” Jean cried out.

The three girls stared in fascination at the window display. In the center, on a golden pedestal, stood a replica of the sacred Garuda bird. It looked magnificent with its eaglelike white head, outstretched red wings, and golden body which seemed more human than birdlike.

"We've found it!" Malee exclaimed exultantly. "My precious bird!"

The three girls hurried into the shop and went up to a male clerk.

Excitedly Malee said, "The Garuda bird in your window. Where did you get it?"

The salesman looked at the girl in annoyance. He drew himself up very tall and replied, "The bird is not for sale at this time."

"How long have you had it?" Jean spoke up.

"I'm not prepared to answer," the clerk replied. "I have already said the bird is not for sale." He turned and began to walk away from them.

Louise moved along the counter, keeping pace with him. "I think it would be to your advantage to answer our questions," she said. "It is very possible that you are displaying stolen property in your window."

At this remark the man stopped walking, wheeled about, and stared at Louise. A look of sudden fear flitted across his face.

"Follow me," he directed.

The three girls were led to the rear of the exclusive shop to the manager's office. The clerk presented the girls and told the manager of Louise's remarks. Then he left.

"Please sit down," the manager requested. "Now tell me just what this is all about."

Malee looked at the Danas, not knowing how much she should tell this stranger. Louise guardedly told enough to convince him that her suspicions were warranted.

"We bought the Garuda bird yesterday from a Far Eastern prince," the manager said.

Instantly the Danas wondered if the Far Eastern prince might be an impostor, perhaps Holden in disguise.

"Was this prince in Oriental dress?" Louise queried.

"Yes, he was," the manager answered. "Why do you ask?"

"I think he may have been masquerading," Louise replied, but did not explain further.

Now Malee spoke up. "I could easily identify the bird you have as mine," she said. "A tiny picture of one of our Thai river boats has been burned into the bamboo on the inside."

The manager pressed a button on his desk. In response to the summons a young man appeared. The manager asked him to bring the bird from the show window. When it arrived, Malee deftly opened the hidden door in the body of the bird and looked inside. A frown of disappointment and bewilderment crossed her forehead.

"Whatever was here has been scraped off. This is exactly where the boat was," she said simply. "But I am sure this bamboo Garuda is mine."

The manager sat in silence a few moments. Finally he said that the shop would remove the bird from display for a period of thirty days.

"By that time something more may have developed," he added graciously. "If this bird belongs to you, it will certainly be returned."

Malee thanked him and said she would let him know the outcome of her search.

"Was there anything inside the bird when you bought it?" Louise inquired.

"Yes, there was," the manager answered. "I'll have it brought here."

The pulses of the three girls began to race. Would the clerk bring in the golden gem-studded Buddha? they wondered.

To their keen disappointment, the article which the salesman presented was golden and cone shaped; it was built in tiers with a segmented spiral top.

"That's a *chedi!*" Malee said. She explained that *chedies* were small buildings erected in front of Thailand temples to hold the ashes of prominent people who were cremated after death.

"You claim this?" the manager asked her.

Malee shook her head. "My bird contained a very different kind of object," she replied. "One more valuable."

Louise, thinking that the thief might have removed the gems from Malee's Buddha statue, asked the manager if the Far Eastern prince had offered any jewels for sale.

"No, he didn't," the manager replied. "And now, young ladies, if you will excuse me—"

The three girls thanked the man for his time and left the shop. On the way back to the hotel, they discussed their discovery in whispers. Malee was positive that the golden Garuda bird was hers, and the Danas were equally positive that Swad Holden was the "Far Eastern prince," and had removed the gold Buddha from the bird. He had probably disposed of the gems in other stores. "Let's try to find out," Louise proposed.

From their hotel room she and Jean took turns phoning jewelry stores, but they had no luck.

"It looks hopeless," Jean said with a sigh.

The girls and Aunt Harriet spent that evening and all the following day attending the theater and sightseeing.

Malee was very enthusiastic. "New York is a wonderful city and so different from mine. Is it not amazing how people of different nations can build so many types of homes in which to live and places in which to work and temples in which to worship, and yet have the same aspirations and love of family and friends?"

"It is indeed," Louise agreed. "And I can hardly wait to see your country."

The following morning the travelers were up early to get to Kennedy International Airport. Uncle Ned accompanied them, and after an exchange of fond farewells and good-luck wishes, the girls and Aunt Harriet boarded their plane to San Francisco.

As soon as the group reached the California city, they taxied to their hotel and registered, but Malee used a pseudonym to avoid publicity. When they were shown to their rooms, Louise said:

"I think we should check with the airline about our flight to Honolulu right away."

The others agreed and Louise put in the call. There was a long pause, then a voice indicated that Louise was getting an answer. She looked puzzled.

"You mean you don't have our names?" she cried out. "We have no seats on the flight to Honolulu?"

CHAPTER VI

# Anonymous Warning

WITH a sigh Louise sat down on her bed in the hotel room. "I can't understand it," she said. "There's been some kind of a mix-up, Malee."

Aunt Harriet looked disturbed. From the start she had been wary of their pursuit of a thief and the danger it involved. This new development concerning their reservations to Honolulu seemed to bear out her misgivings.

Malee was very pale but said nothing. She seemed completely baffled.

Suddenly Jean snapped her fingers. "I have an idea," she said. "Malee, since we were trying to keep this trip sort of a secret, maybe the reservations are being held in the name of your cousin."

"Oh, Jean, that must be it!" Malee exclaimed. She asked Louise to phone again.

This time Louise mentioned the cousin's name and was told that no information could be given over the telephone. The reservation clerk said that if she came to the airline's ticket office and identified herself, he was sure that her question would be answered.

"Please let us hurry," Malee urged. "I must find out what this is all about."

Aunt Harriet did not think it necessary for her to accompany the girls and decided to rest while they were gone.

When they reached the airline's office, the girls showed their passports and Aunt Harriet's. The young clerk smiled and went into another office. He returned immediately with an envelope containing the reservations.

"The Thai Embassy in Washington asked us to handle the matter this way," he said. His eyes twinkled. "Sounds as if there might be a mystery going on."

The three girls smiled but neither affirmed nor denied his statement. They thanked him and left the ticket office. Malee took her two friends by the arm and said:

"You see how I need you girls? I probably never would have thought of asking for the reservations under another name."

Jean chuckled. "We've done pretty well so far, but don't praise us too highly. The mystery of your bamboo bird has not yet been solved."

Nevertheless, Malee was in a gay mood. She asked the girls to go shopping with her for gifts to take to her mother, sister, and father. "I suppose

I should buy gifts for all my family, but there are so many of them, it would take too long."

Malee explained that the Wongsuwan household, like many in Thailand, included several relatives—her sister's husband, a widowed aunt of Mrs. Wongsuwan, and her father's younger brother.

"You must have a very big house," Jean remarked.

Louise was thinking that the Danas would want to present their host and hostess with gifts. "Guess I'll call Aunt Harriet and consult her about what to buy," she decided.

Louise excused herself, stepped into a telephone booth, and called the hotel. Her aunt suggested that because of the luggage-weight problem, it would be wise to select something light.

"It's hard to think of anything which the Wongsuwans may not have and which would be useful," Aunt Harriet went on. "But leave it to me. I'll take care of it."

Later, when the girls returned to the hotel, Aunt Harriet found a chance to speak to her nieces alone. "I have the gift." It was a luncheon set.

"It's simply gorgeous!" exclaimed Jean. "The Wongsuwans should love it!"

The travelers were taking a jet plane for Honolulu the following evening, so they spent the morning and afternoon sightseeing.

When the tour was over, Jean asked Malee, "Did you know that San Franciso has been nicknamed the Rome of the United States? It's built on seven hills."

"It is a most beautiful and exciting place," Malee remarked, then she added with a laugh, "The taxi drivers are marvelous the way they rush up and down the hills. I must confess I was scared several times."

"What did you like best?" Aunt Harriet asked.

Malee giggled. "The seals."

"Oh, those seals out on the ocean rocks beyond the park are very famous," Aunt Harriet told her. "They are such carefree clowns. They're always frolicking, except when they're barking for food."

Later, aboard the plane for Honolulu, the girls looked down at the city, which was a myriad of twinkling lights.

"Isn't the Golden Gate Bridge fascinating?" Louise observed. "It's about the longest bridge in the world."

Early the next morning the travelers reached Honolulu. As they stepped from the plane and walked toward the gate, Malee and her friends were met by several smiling young women who hung leis of plumeria around their necks. The delicate flowers smelled deliciously sweet.

"Why, thank you," the Danas said together, and Malee added, "It is very kind of you."

"We hope you will enjoy your stay on the islands," said one of the young women, who was wearing an airline uniform.

A look of amazement came over Malee's face. Then she put her palms together, as if in an attitude of prayer, and began to bow and smile, as was the custom of greeting in Thailand.

The Danas followed her glance and realized that she had recognized a man and woman who were hurrying toward her. As the man dropped a lei about the Thai girl's neck, she cried out:

"Noi!" Turning to the young woman, she exclaimed, "Bua!"

They greeted one another affectionately, then Malee said, "I should like you to meet my very dear friends, the Danas. This is Miss Dana, this is Louise, and here is Jean." To the Danas she said, "These are my friends from Bangkok, the Punyarachoons, now living in Honolulu."

"We are delighted to meet you," said Noi. He and his wife dropped leis of purple Vanda orchids about the necks of Louise, Jean, and their aunt.

"This is a most unexpected reception," Aunt Harriet said. "Thank you both very much."

Puzzled, Malee asked, "How did you know we were coming?"

Mr. and Mrs. Punyarachoon showed surprise. "You mean you did not know we would meet you?" Noi asked.

Malee said they knew nothing about it. The trip actually was supposed to be a secret.

Noi told her that a cable had been hand-delivered to him. The message was from the Thai Embassy in

Washington and had requested him to meet the visitors and show them every hospitality.

"As they instructed, I canceled your reservation at the hotel. You will stay with us."

Aunt Harriet demurred. "That is very kind of you, but we don't want to impose. Perhaps Malee should stay with you. My nieces and I can go to the hotel."

Bua smiled understandingly. "Our home is large and we have several servants. It would delight us very much if you would be our guests. Friends of Malee's are friends of ours also."

Aunt Harriet accepted graciously, then they all went to claim their baggage. Noi asked for the luggage checks, which he in turn handed to his chauffeur. The Punyarachoons led the way to their large car.

Not a word was said about Malee's mystery during the drive to the Punyarachoon estate, and the Danas wondered how much their host and hostess knew. They eagerly watched all the interesting sights of Honolulu as they rode—beautiful Waikiki Beach with its skyscraper hotels, the statue of the famous King Kamehameha, and the old palace in the park.

"This palace," said Noi, "is the only real palace anywhere in the United States."

The home which the Punyarachoons were renting while Noi was transacting business in the islands was located in the Diamond Head area. On the way, the girls saw palm and hau and monkey-pod trees. Red and yellow hibiscus bloomed in profusion and there were whole hedges of tiny orchids!

"Hawaii must be a heavenly place to live," Louise remarked as they turned into the driveway of their host's estate.

"Yes, it is, and in many ways it reminds us of Bangkok," Bua replied.

The car stopped at the front door of the large, English-type stucco mansion. As the guests entered, Bua said, "I hope you will be happy during your stay here. Please, as you Americans say, make yourselves at home. Do whatever you might do in your own home. A maid will show you to your rooms. I am sure you will want to change to cooler dresses. Then please come down to breakfast."

The rooms were large and comfortably furnished, with heavily carved Victorian pieces. After quick baths and a change of clothes, Malee and the Danas went downstairs.

The breakfast of pineapple slices, juicy and sweet, with eggs and toast, was served on a patio shaded by a large hau tree. A long lawn swept away from the house down toward a pool bordered by tropical trees and bushes.

"If you listen carefully," Bua said, "you can hear the ocean surf pounding against the lava rock on the beach."

"Oh, yes, I can," Louise replied.

To one side of the garden was a summerhouse and beyond this a small building which looked like a tool shed.

"Shall we go sightseeing today?" Bua suggested.

The morning and afternoon were spent in the country where the visitors were fascinated by the huge sugar-cane and pineapple plantations. That evening dinner was served in the spacious dining room, then the Punyarachoons led their guests out to the patio. So far, no word had been mentioned about the mystery, but now Bua whispered to the girls:

"I should like to learn more about the theft of the bamboo bird. I think it best if none of the servants overhears us. Suppose we stroll out on the lawn and you tell me."

Instantly Malee asked, "How did you hear about the bird?"

"That is a mystery in itself," Bua replied. "We received a warning phone call last night. The speaker would not give his name, but told us all about the bird and the golden Buddha with the gems. He suggested that Malee might be in danger and to keep her and her friends at home this evening."

"Oh, what did he mean by that?" Malee asked fearfully.

"I do not know, and furthermore we have no idea who the person was." Bua turned questioningly to the Danas.

"I can make a guess," Louise said. "I think the cable you received was a fake. Somebody wanted Malee to be here rather than at a hotel for some sinister reason, I'm sure. The phone call was a follow-up to be sure you would keep her here this evening."

"In that case," Noi said with determination, "I shall see to it that no one enters these grounds."

He pressed a button on the house wall to summon the butler. Turning to his wife, he said, "Bua, tell Sam to get the gardener, and instruct them both to walk around the outside of our grounds. Have them stop anyone trying to get in. I'll go down beyond the pond and watch that area." He turned and hurried away.

Sam appeared and immediately rushed off when Bua gave him the message. The group on the patio continued to discuss this latest phase of the mystery.

"Oh, dear!" said Malee. "It seems as if everywhere I go I get other people into trouble."

The words were hardly out of her mouth when they heard a yell from just beyond the pond. This was followed by a shout and a scream. The listeners tensed. Had someone attacked Noi, or had he captured an intruder?

CHAPTER VII

# Capturing an Intruder

FEAR rooted the Danas and their friends to the spot for a moment. But Louise and Jean quickly recovered and sped toward the area in back of the pond.

But Louise stopped Jean. "We shouldn't leave Malee unprotected," she cautioned. "I have a feeling this whole thing is a decoy, maybe to kidnap her."

Jean agreed, and the sisters turned back. "I have a plan," Louise said. "Leave it to me."

She took Malee by the hand and pulled her toward the tool shed the Danas had noticed earlier. Louise whispered, "Malee, you'd better hide in here if it's open."

To the girls' relief, there was a key in the lock. Swiftly Louise yanked the door open. She made sure no one was inside, then gently pushed Malee in.

"Don't make a sound," Louise warned her friend.

She quietly closed the door, locked it, and pocketed the key.

Turning, she saw that Jean, Bua, Aunt Harriet, and two women servants were hurrying across the lawn in the direction of the scream.

"This means nobody is guarding the house," Louise told herself. "That might be the very thing Malee's enemies want!"

She hurried back toward the house and began to circle it. Suddenly, in the dim light from the windows, she saw a ladder planted against a second-floor window.

*A man was climbing it!*

Louise wondered what she should do. With no one around to help her, she had little chance of stopping the intruder. "If I cry out," she thought, "he may escape." Louise was sure that he was connected with the Thailand mysteries. "If we could only capture him, they might be solved right now!"

To Louise's relief, she saw the chauffeur coming toward her. Now was her chance! Rushing to the foot of the ladder, she called to the man above, "Stop!"

The intruder looked down at her, then disappeared through the window into the second floor of the house.

"He may get away through one of the doors before we can stop him!" Louise thought worriedly. "I can't possibly guard all the doors."

She ran to the chauffeur and told him about the

intruder. "I'll get the gardener and we will try to watch all the doors," he said. "Miss Dana, will you use the phone in the garage to call the police?"

As Louise ran toward the garage, she met Noi, Jean, and Bua returning to the house. "You weren't hurt?" she asked Noi.

"No, but somebody—" He broke off. "I'll tell you later. I can see something is wrong. What is it, Louise?"

"There's an intruder in your house. I'm going to the garage to call the police. I suggest you all surround the house, so that you can catch the man if he comes out. And don't mention Malee's name. I'll explain about that later."

"Right," Noi agreed.

Louise sped off. As she neared the garage, the young sleuth wondered if another mysterious intruder might be inside, hiding behind a car, so she switched on the wall light and looked around before entering. After assuring herself that no one was there, she phoned the Honolulu police.

"I'll send some men up immediately," the officer promised.

By the time Louise got back to the house, she found it completely surrounded by the Punyarachoons and their servants, as well as Aunt Harriet and Jean.

"The man is still in there," Jean said. "I caught a glimpse of his shadow upstairs when he passed near a light."

Although it seemed like an eternity to the waiting group, it was actually only a few minutes before a police car roared up the driveway and four officers ran up to them. Noi quickly explained what had happened and the policemen entered the house. Those outside waited breathlessly. Five minutes went by. Ten.

"Oh, maybe that dreadful man got away!" Bua said in disappointment.

Just then one of the officers came to the front door and called everyone inside. Two of the policemen were holding a cowering young Asiatic. He refused to give his name or address or reason for entry. He would only say he was not guilty of any wrongdoing. He had not yelled or screamed and had taken nothing from the house.

"You'll come along with us and stay in jail until you talk," one of the officers said.

After the young intruder had been led away by two of the policemen, Louise told the rest of the group that she had locked Malee in the tool shed to protect her. "We'd better get her," she said.

Noi and one of the policemen went with Louise. Malee was unharmed but badly frightened. She wanted to know what had happened.

Louise told her about the intruder and explained why she had locked her in. Malee said plaintively that again she was sorry to have caused trouble for everyone.

"Trouble!" Noi said. "I am so thankful you are

safe. It is very exasperating not to know what this is all about. Apparently someone is determined to keep you and your friends from going to Bangkok. Well, he shall not do it! I shall have guards placed around the house continually during your stay here."

"You are a true friend," Malee said gratefully.

As soon as they reached the house, Noi asked one of the officers if he would make arrangements for a police guard to protect the estate for the night. "I'll do so immediately," he replied.

The fourth policeman remained at the house. He pulled out a notebook and asked for full details of what had happened up to the time the police had reached the Punyarachoons'.

Noi told his story first. "I was standing behind the hedge when suddenly I heard footsteps not far away. I turned quickly and was just in time to keep a man from hitting me on the head. I made an attempt to grab him, but he evidently became scared, because he ran off quickly. I went after him, but he disappeared. A few seconds later I heard the yell and the shout. I am sure he made them. I cannot understand why, if he was trying to escape, he gave away his position."

Louise spoke up. "I think it was to draw attention to that area and give the other intruder a chance to get into the house."

"I see," said Noi. He heaved a sigh. "I am most thankful that all their plans failed."

Malee offered to leave and stay at a hotel. The Danas echoed the suggestion, but the Punyarachoons would not hear of this. In a short while the police guard appeared.

Aunt Harriet was exhausted and excused herself. Malee, too, said she felt very much like being alone and resting. It was not long before everyone had gone to bed. Louise and Jean, sharing a bed in a large, airy room, whispered for a long time.

"I feel," Louise declared, "that something much bigger is involved than just the stealing of Malee's bamboo bird."

"Yes, there must be," Jean agreed. "The question is what?"

"It has me puzzled," Louise confessed.

After a while the sisters came to the conclusion that Swad Holden was probably engineering the whole thing.

"He may be right here in Honolulu," Louise surmised. "He could even have been the person who tried to attack Noi."

Jean agreed. "I think the police should be notified about Mr. Holden. And it's my guess that he's on his way to Bangkok, too, and is trying to keep Malee from returning there. Maybe the police could arrest him at the airport before he leaves Hawaii."

Jean got up, put on her robe and slippers, and said she would go to the telephone in the downstairs hall and call headquarters. "I'll give them the description of Swad Holden we got from Mrs. Randolph and Uncle Ned and the steward on the *Balaska*."

"And don't forget to tell the police," Louise suggested, "that Swad Holden is apt to be in disguise."

"I'll do that," said Jean as she tiptoed from the room.

Louise fully expected her sister to return within five minutes. But ten minutes went by and still no Jean. "She must be having a long conversation with the police," Louise thought.

When twenty minutes had gone by and Jean still had not returned, Louise became alarmed.

"There may be another intruder hiding in this house! Maybe he wouldn't let Jean phone! She could be a prisoner!" Louise thought fearfully.

She got up and hurried downstairs to find Jean.

CHAPTER VIII

# "*Chun Pood Thai Mai Dai*"

WHEN Louise reached the first floor, it was very quiet. No one was at the hall telephone. Moonlight streamed through the windows, and guided Louise from room to room.

"Jean?" she called softly.

With pulses throbbing, Louise tiptoed through the first-floor rooms. At every step she wondered if someone might pounce out at her from the shadows, and she tried to look in all directions at once. There was complete silence and still no sign of Jean.

Finally Louise had covered every room except the kitchen. Turning a corner of the hall, she noticed a rim of light around the swinging kitchen door. Cautiously, Louise pushed open the door. She gave a great sigh of relief and burst into laughter.

Jean Dana was about to pick up a tray from a table. On the tray was a plate of sandwiches and two glasses of milk.

"Jean!" Louise said in a loud whisper. "You scared me silly!"

"How come?" her sister asked in surprise.

"Do you know how long you've been gone from our room? Over twenty minutes!"

"Sorry I worried you. After I called the police, I felt so hungry I decided to come out here. Bua told us to make ourselves at home, you know. I guess all the excitement gave me a midnight appetite."

Louise giggled. "Now that you mention it, I'm starving too."

The girls crept up the stairway and went back to their room. They ate the sandwiches and drank the milk, then climbed into bed again. Jean and Louise slept soundly until after eight the next morning. They apologized for being late for breakfast and told of their raid on the refrigerator.

Bua smiled. "I am glad you helped yourself," she said.

Malee and the Danas were to fly to Japan that afternoon. The travelers spent the balance of the morning talking with Bua and Noi.

Louise telephoned the police just before leaving the house for the airport. She learned that Swad Holden had not been found, and that the prisoner had maintained a stubborn silence.

"If we have any news for you, Miss Dana," the chief said, "I'll report it to the Punyarachoons and they in turn can notify you wherever you are."

Later, when the travelers were en route to Tokyo, Malee, who was seated with Louise just ahead of Aunt Harriet and Jean, turned and leaned sidewise against the back of her seat.

"Would you all like to hear a little about the history of my country?" she inquired.

"Oh, yes," the Danas answered.

"Like the United States," Malee began, "present-day Thailand is made up of different races. As in your country, people travel there from various lands. It is thought that the original Thai migrated from the Yunnan Province of China over a thousand years ago. They came down hunting for fertile lands and spread out through Laos, Cambodia, and my country, which used to be called Siam.

"On the way, some of them stopped at the great city of Angkor in Cambodia. This was inhabited by the Khmers from India. They had a magnificent palace and many temples. The Thai and Khmers intermarried. Later, the city was damaged in war and abandoned. The jungle grew up around it.

"But a great many of the buildings have now been uncovered, and I hope while you are visiting Thailand you can fly over there and see them."

"It sounds fascinating," Louise remarked.

"I suppose many wars in history have been started for foolish reasons," Malee went on. "But one which took place between the country of Burma and my people would take a prize. It was called 'The War of the White Elephant.' "

Malee explained that white elephants indicated power, and only kings could own them. Just before the war, the King of Siam owned seven white elephants and one of his jealous neighbors decided to take them for himself.

"You mean that there was actually war between the two countries over that little herd of elephants?" Jean questioned.

"That is the truth," Malee replied. "Have you ever read *Anna and the King of Siam?*" The Danas said they had seen a play based on the story.

"It is a true story, except for the romantic part," Malee went on. "The Siamese king sent for the English governess to teach his children. His son, Chulalongkorn, was one of our beloved rulers, and his son after him.

"The king who sent for Anna was named Mongkut. He is reputed to have been a tyrant, but he did much good for our country. Great Britain and the United States took a great interest in Siam after that. We are all good friends now.

"In 1932 our government was changed from an absolute monarchy to a constitutional monarchy. I am happy to say that Thailand never has any want. We are very fortunate to have plenty of rain which provides water for our rice crops, so no one is ever hungry."

After Malee had finished, Louise remarked that when Malee spoke in Thai, it seemed almost as if she were singing. "Do all your people speak this way?" Louise asked.

Malee laughed. "I suppose you might say that we do. This is because a word in our language has different meanings depending on whether you speak it in a high voice, a medium tone, or a low key. Let me teach you a few phrases. Now repeat after me: *Chun pood Thai mai dai.*"

The Danas tried several times but could not catch Malee's inflection exactly. "That is good enough," she said. "People will understand you. You were saying 'I cannot speak Thai.'"

Aunt Harriet asked what expressions they might need while shopping. Malee told her that practically all shopkeepers in Bangkok speak very good English. But one phrase which might help the Americans was "*Tao rai*—how much?"

"What are the names of Thai currency?" Aunt Harriet inquired.

"Everything is based on the baht," Malee answered.

"That makes it easy." Louise laughed.

"I bought something for a baht," Jean joked.

The next bit of excitement came when the girls were told they were losing a day because they were crossing the international date line. Once more they turned their watches back and Jean facetiously remarked that they had certainly traveled a good many miles but were always gaining time.

"It's just the reverse," Aunt Harriet said. "We've lost a whole day! One minute ago it was Thursday. Now it's Friday!"

Malee laughed. "By the time you reach Thailand, you will be exactly halfway around the world time-wise. Midnight in Bangkok will be noonday in New York."

Being weary, the three girls fell asleep. When they were awake again, Aunt Harriet leaned forward and told Malee that she had been thinking about their stay in Bangkok and had decided it would be best if she and her nieces went to a hotel rather than inconvenience the Wongsuwans.

"Oh, Miss Dana, my parents and I are counting on your visit." Malee went on to say they would do everything to make the Americans' stay comfortable and happy.

In the meantime, Aunt Harriet had been writing a notation on a pad. When Malee was not looking, she passed the note to Jean. It read:

"*I hear the city is overrun with little lizards. I know they're necessary to eat insects, but I don't like them. They surely won't be in a modern, air-conditioned hotel, but they may be in Malee's home!*"

Jean could hardly stifle a giggle, but she came to her aunt's defense and said, "Malee, please don't think we're not appreciative of your invitation. It might be better for any enemy of yours to think that we Danas have merely come to Bangkok on a sightseeing and not a sleuthing trip."

Louise, who sensed that Aunt Harriet had a sound reason for her suggestion, in turn backed up Jean and her supposition. She added, "We may be able to do even better detective work for you if we're not at your home. Let's try it that way, anyhow."

Malee finally consented and said, "We shall take you to the Oriental Hotel and ask for a river-front room in the new air-conditioned wing. You will like it there. And perhaps you will have a better chance to watch the fascinating life on the Menam Chao Phraya. That's the name of the principal river which we in Thailand think of as our main street."

At last the travelers reached Tokyo. There was a short wait for the Bangkok flight. Because of this the Dana group was requested by the officials to remain in the airport building. After showing their passports, they were permitted to enter the large, modern waiting room.

The Danas, who had never been to Japan, were fascinated by women in kimonos and obis hurrying along with friends in Occidental dress. Most of the men and children wore Western-style clothes. The private school students were dressed in uniforms—the boys in tight-fitting black suits and the girls in navy-blue skirts and middy blouses.

"Isn't this interesting!" Jean said to her sister, as she gazed around at the people who bowed continuously in greeting instead of shaking hands.

"Let's walk around a little," Louise suggested.

When they reached the far end of the great waiting room, a voice suddenly spoke over the loudspeaker, first in Japanese, then in singsong English. The girls stood electrified, as they heard the message.

"Mees-taire Holden please report at once to JAL ticket coun-taire."

"*Holden!*" Louise exclaimed. "We must find him at once!"

Quickly the girls located a seat for Aunt Harriet, piled up their hand luggage at her side, then dashed off toward the Japan Air Lines ticket counter.

CHAPTER IX

# An Airport Mix-up

THE three girls had difficulty making their way to the Japan Air Lines ticket counter. It was a good distance away and the waiting room was crowded. There seemed to be many *bon voyage* parties, with the Japanese bowing low and offering *presentos* to the departing travelers. The farewell gifts were being tied into gaily colored cloth squares called *furoshiki*.

"Oh, Mr. Holden may be gone before we can get there!" Jean fretted. "And if he *is* Swad Holden—"

At last the trio drew near the counter. Three stocky, dark-haired men stood there. All wore hats, so it was impossible to determine whether or not their hair was slicked down.

"Let's separate and each of us cover one of the men," Louise directed. "Get as close as you can, Malee, and listen to the conversation."

Louise had hardly planted herself near the man

she was to watch, when the clerk said, "We have a cancellation, Mr. Holden."

"Very good," the man replied, then began speaking in a foreign tongue which Louise assumed was Japanese. Instantly she reflected that Swad Holden was a linguist and a world traveler. He probably could speak Japanese!

As Mr. Holden turned from the counter, Louise got a good look at him. He was a rather nice-looking, pleasant person—and not at all what she thought of as the underhanded, scheming type. Nevertheless, Louise felt she should find out his first name.

Smiling, she said to him, "I beg your pardon but my friends and I"—she indicated Jean and Malee—"have a message for a certain Mr. Holden. We have never met him and wondered if you might be the man. Would you mind telling me your first name?"

Mr. Holden laughed. "I'll be jolly glad to," he replied in a clipped British accent. "Horrible name, though. It's Thaddeus."

"Thank you very much," Louise said, trying to think of some way to keep the man talking. She felt that he might still be Swad Holden attempting to elude her by using a false first name.

But the man was saying, "And now, if you will excuse me, I must hurry. If I do not go through Customs immediately, I will miss my plane."

Louise could think of no valid excuse to continue

the conversation. But why had he not asked the full name of the other Holden?

"I guess he's not Swad, and so he's not interested," she decided. Aloud Louise said, "Please forgive me for delaying you. It must be someone else I'm looking for."

Jean and Malee had learned that the two men they were watching were not named Holden. And neither fitted the description Mrs. Randolph and the steward had given.

After Louise had told her story, Jean giggled. "I'll bet Mr. Thaddeus Holden thought you were looking for a date!" she teased.

"All right, all right," Louise answered. "But I'll find the right Mr. Holden yet and you can bet I won't make a date with *him!*"

Malee laughed as the three girls made their way back toward Aunt Harriet. Suddenly they heard shouts in Japanese and saw two men, each carrying a suitcase, running very fast in their direction. For a second, Louise and Jean thought the men might be calling to them, but then they realized that the two were racing to catch a plane and were asking people to get out of the way.

The girls pulled back with the rest of the crowd, but a little old lady in a black kimono, her back to the men, was trudging along on high platform sandals. She seemed completely oblivious of the warning. The men, in turn, must have expected her to move aside, because they did not slow down.

Jean, foreseeing a possible accident, dashed forward to help the elderly woman out of the way. But the Japanese woman did not understand and pulled back. At that instant one of the running men crashed into Jean. The suitcase flew from his hand and both he and Jean fell to the floor.

The second man, trying to stop short, had bumped into Louise and Malee. When they regained their balance, and Jean and the first man were on their feet, there were profuse apologies. The two Japanese, their heels together, bowed from the waist and repeated:

"So sorry! So sorry!"

Then they picked up their bags and hurried toward the doorway leading to their waiting plane. The little old lady, finally understanding what the commotion was all about, also began to bow and talk in Japanese, smiling in appreciation. The girls could do nothing more than smile in return. They left her and made their way back to Aunt Harriet.

"This language barrier may get us into lots of trouble!" Louise observed.

Aunt Harriet laughed when she heard of the girls' adventure.

Louise was expressing her disappointment at not finding Swad Holden when a man jumped up from a nearby bench and came over to them. He was one of the three men who had been at the JAL ticket counter.

"Pardon me. I could not help but overhear what

Jean dashed forward to help the elderly woman.

you ladies were saying. You are looking for a man named *Swad* Holden?"

"Yes," Louise answered. "Why?"

"Perhaps I can help you. While I was trying to change my reservations for a future flight at another counter, I heard a Japanese talking with the ticket clerk. The name mentioned in the conversation was Swad Holden. I recalled it because it's so unusual. I do not know what they were saying, but I'll be glad to point out the clerk."

The Danas and Malee were excited. They thanked the man and said they would appreciate his help. When they reached the counter and Louise asked about Mr. Swad Holden, the clerk was evasive. "We do not give out any information about our passengers except to officials," he said.

For a moment the Danas were stumped. Then Jean had an idea. She asked, "Was the man who talked about Swad Holden a detective?"

The airline clerk looked at her in amazement, then finally replied, "Yes, he was."

"I'm not surprised," Jean went on. "Confidentially, we are looking for Mr. Swad Holden because we think he may have stolen something which belongs to our friend." She touched Malee's arm.

"That is very serious," the man remarked. "I think you should notify the Tokyo police. I can tell you this, however. Mr. Swad Holden *was* here, but he has left Japan."

CHAPTER X

# Police Interview

THE Danas and Malee stared at one another in vexation. Swad Holden had eluded them! The airline clerk smilingly refused to tell them the man's destination, and the girls turned away from the counter.

"Perhaps we should get in touch with the Tokyo police," Louise said thoughtfully.

"But we have only three-quarters of an hour before departure," Jean pointed out.

"Just the same, I feel that we should report what we know."

Jean's eyes wandered back to the airline clerk. "Maybe we can get him to help us some more," she said.

Hopefully she went back to the counter and said with a smile, "We're going to take your advice and call the police, but we don't speak your language. Could you possibly help us?"

A big grin spread over the Japanese clerk's face.

"I shall be most happy to assist you. I am just finishing my work here. Shall we go to a telephone booth?"

Jean accepted his offer and the three girls hurried along beside him. He put in the call, and was told that two Japanese detectives would arrive in a few minutes and meet them at this spot. Actually it was fifteen minutes before the detectives entered the terminal and found the group.

To the girls' delight, the two officers, who were not in uniform, spoke excellent English. They explained that they worked for Interpol.

"Do you know what that is?" one of them asked.

"Yes," Louise answered. "The International Police Organization which keeps track of international criminals."

"Please tell us all you know about Mr. Swad Holden," the other officer urged.

Louise related the full story. Then, to her amazement, the men said they already knew it from Interpol.

"Swad Holden is suspected of many thefts in various countries," the officer added. "But nothing has been proved against him yet."

Jean asked if the two men would mind telling her how they had learned of the stolen bamboo Garuda bird and the golden Buddha.

"From the New York police," the first officer replied. "The jeweler who talked with you young ladies reported it."

"Did he mention the Far Eastern prince who sold the bird to him and the chedi that was in it?" Louise asked.

"Yes, but we have no idea who this prince is. Perhaps you do?" The officer's eyes twinkled.

Malee spoke up. "My friends are wonderful sleuths. They think he was Swad Holden in disguise."

Now it was the detectives' turn to look amazed. They said it was a very good deduction indeed and asked the girls to contact their organization if they came upon any further important information.

Louise promised they would, then added, "Now that you know why we're trying to find Swad Holden, perhaps you will tell us what his next destination is?"

The airline clerk finally relented. "It is Bangkok."

"That is where we are going!" Malee explained.

Just then the loud-speaker summoned the passengers for the flight to Bangkok. There were hurried good-bys to the detectives and the clerk, and the girls went at once to rejoin Aunt Harriet.

"Where in the world have you been?" she asked, gathering up her handbag, a tote bag, a magazine, and a couple of books.

"We have lots of exciting things to tell you, but let's wait until we get on the plane," Louise said hurriedly.

Aunt Harriet, her nieces, and Malee were seated

across the aisle from one another in the huge plane. This time Malee sat with Aunt Harriet, and told her of the meeting with the men from Interpol.

Meanwhile, Louise and Jean were looking at the passengers as they came aboard. They were of many different nationalities. All of the men wore Western-style suits, but those from India had full beards and turbans.

The women, however, were in native attire—some of the Japanese in kimonos, the Chinese in black satin trousers with embroidered satin coats, and the women from India in filmy, bright-colored saris.

Louise leaned across the aisle and said to Malee, "Aren't the costumes beautiful and interesting? Are there any here from your country?"

Malee smiled. "No. Thailand has had British influence for so long that in public we wear the same type clothes you do. We use the old traditional costumes only on the stage or in our dance performances."

About an hour later a meal was served on trays to the passengers. Louise said to her sister, "How does the airline manage to satisfy the tastes of people from so many countries?"

Jean shrugged. When her own tray arrived, she noticed how cleverly this had been done. The meal included plain rice, pieces of chicken, chunks of pork, a vegetable salad, a cup of custard, and an array of tiny covered dishes. The sisters peeked into these, but could not figure out what the contents were. They appealed to Malee for an explanation.

"They are sauces to please all tastes," she replied, smiling. "Some are very hot curries, others are bland. One of these is cranberry jelly."

Aunt Harriet and her nieces watched Malee in fascination as she dipped spoonfuls of rice into first one curry, then another. Finally Jean decided to try one of them.

"Don't take much of it," Malee warned.

Jean thought she was being careful, but a moment later her eyes began to blink and tear, and she started to cough.

"I'm burning up!"

As Jean reached hastily for her cup of water, Malee warned, "Do not drink that! It will only make you feel worse. Wait a few moments and the burning sensation will go away."

To Jean's relief, this is exactly what happened. But she decided not to try any of the other curries. Malee pointed out the milder sauces to Aunt Harriet and Louise, and they found them delicious.

Later on, Louise and Jean talked quietly about the mystery they were trying to solve. "Apparently we're not after any ordinary thief," Louise observed. "Do you suppose someone in Malee's family might have some connection with Mr. Holden's scheme?"

"I don't know," Jean answered, "but I do think

Malee suspects someone, which is the secret she hasn't told us. I have a hunch that she's embarrassed to talk about it."

"You're probably right," Louise agreed.

"I'm not going to prod her about it," said Jean. "It will be enough for me to find out what became of Malee's gold Buddha."

As the great plane circled for a landing, the travelers saw a fairyland city glistening in the sunlight. Everywhere golden cone-shaped spires of temples rose into the sky. The gold, Malee told them, was mixed with bits of gay pottery and colored glass which glittered like sparkling gems. Besides the temples and the chedies, there were stately public buildings, beautiful homes with gardens, and more modest houses of natural wood. The main streets were crisscrossed with tree-shaded canals.

"Those are the *klongs*," Malee said.

"What a magnificent city!" Louise burst out.

Jean whispered excitedly to her sister, "Somewhere below us, among all that grandeur, is the thief who stole the bamboo bird."

## CHAPTER XI

# A Surprising Request

AUNT HARRIET and the three girls felt the warm, caressing sunshine of the tropical city as they came out of the plane. A happy smile spread over Malee's face. Starting down the stairway, she cried out gaily:

"I see my mother and father and sister. Oh, and there is my brother-in-law."

A few minutes later greetings and introductions were exchanged. The Danas thought they had never seen a more attractive family group than the Wongsuwans. All were handsome, olive-skinned, smiling people. The brother-in-law's name was Boonruang Kinaree, but Malee said his nickname was Boonmi. He was about twenty-eight years old, medium height, and very slender. He did not smile and seemed quite formal.

His pretty wife, Pratoom, twenty-two, was very different. She bowed graciously and acted extremely glad to see the visitors. When Malee announced that the Danas had decided to stay at a hotel, Pratoom became quite upset.

"We were looking forward to having you stay with us," she said.

Instantly Boonmi spoke up. "No doubt Miss Dana and her nieces will be more comfortable at the Oriental Hotel," he said. "And there they can order American food which they would prefer, I am sure."

Louise and Jean had the feeling that Boonmi was not eager to have the Danas visit the Wongsuwans. Malee's secret flashed through their minds. Did she suspect that her brother-in-law might have something to do with causing the complication which Malee had mentioned?

Mrs. Wongsuwan spoke up. "We shall respect your wishes, Miss Dana, of course," she said. "But we shall miss the opportunity to make you one of our family group while you are in Bangkok."

Her husband smiled understandingly also. "You will find the customs in our two countries quite different. I trust that you will permit us to show you the many things in Bangkok of which we are so proud."

"That would be wonderful," Aunt Harriet said warmly.

Malee's father asked for the luggage checks, then he led the way into the airport terminal and handed the stubs to the man who, he said, was Nai Samret, the family chauffeur. The visitors were escorted to a desk where they showed their passports and turned in three photographs each. Next they had to present their health certificates proving that they had had all the required inoculations, then they were given disembarkation cards.

During the long drive from the airport into the heart of Bangkok, the visitors were intrigued with the extensive rice fields. Mr. Wongsuwan explained that there were two crops of the grain a year.

"We have three seasons," he continued. "It's hot from March to May and rainy from June to October. At the end of this time all the fields have been flooded anew and we are ready for a second planting. From November to February is our cool season, but you will find it around seventy-five to eighty degrees."

"We came at just the right time," Jean said, smiling.

"Yes, you did."

When they reached the Oriental Hotel, only Mr. Wongsuwan and Malee went inside with the Danas. He arranged for the best accommodations, then said good-by and returned to the car.

Malee went up in the elevator with her friends. A smiling bellboy in an immaculate white suit led them along a concrete porch, then down a short flight of inside steps. At the foot were two doors leading into separate rooms. He unlocked them, then carried Aunt Harriet's luggage into one room, the sisters' into the other.

Malee led Louise and Jean to the large picture window in their room. From there, they had a fine view of the river.

There were many kinds of boats, some propelled by motors but most of them by people who stood at one end and poled their craft.

"Those boats with the rounded roof over part of them—are they the sampans?" Louise asked.

"Yes," Malee replied. "And to many people they are home."

"You mean people live on them?"

"On the bigger ones, yes," Malee answered, then she excused herself. "I do not want to keep my family waiting. I will phone you very soon. And we shall make some plans for sightseeing."

After their friend had gone, the Danas unlocked their bags and began to unpack. Some of their dresses were very wrinkled.

"We'd better have these pressed," Louise suggested.

Jean turned to the door just as her aunt entered. The girls showed her the rumpled clothing. "We'll ring for the boy," she suggested. "Also, when he comes, please tell him that the bulb in the lamp on my desk is out."

The smiling young man appeared very quickly. Although all he said was "Yes, madam," the Danas felt that he understood about the dresses. Then Jean told him about the lamp bulb. He nodded, smiled, and went off.

In two minutes he returned, carrying a Thermos jug of ice water which he set on the sisters' desk. Since there already was one there and Aunt Harriet said there was a pitcher in her room, the Danas assumed he had not understood about the lamp bulb.

Jean said to him, "No, no. Lamp, bulb." Then she pointed to Aunt Harriet and the bedroom beyond.

Once more the boy disappeared but soon returned. This time he carried a lamp, which he set on a low table in the girls' room. He carried the cord across to a wall socket. Smiling as if pleased he had at last comprehended, he bowed low and left.

The three Danas tried hard not to giggle. Finally Aunt Harriet said jokingly, "I hope he didn't misunderstand about your dresses, girls. Who knows? You may receive some Siamese costumes in return!"

She suggested that after bathing and changing their clothes, they all take a walk and do some window shopping.

When they were ready, Louise said, "I'd like to talk with the police. They may know if Swad Holden has come to Bangkok."

"I think we'd better ask for directions to police headquarters at the desk," her aunt suggested.

When they reached the first floor, Louise asked the room clerk to direct her to the police. A horrified look came over his face.

"The police!" he repeated. "Please do not call the police! Please tell me what is the trouble with our accommodations. I will rectify any mistake at once."

A second misunderstanding within a few minutes! This time the Danas could not refrain from laughing.

"Please forgive us," said Aunt Harriet. "We find your accommodations excellent. We have no fault to find with your hotel. Our reason for wishing to talk to the police concerns a different matter."

"I see. I am sorry for my mistake. I was too hasty," the clerk apologized.

He said that he himself would get in touch with the police department and ask that an officer who spoke English come to the hotel to talk to the Danas. "Shall I request him to be here in half an hour?" the man wanted to know.

"That will be fine," Louise said. "Thank you."

The shopping district was just a short walk from the hotel. The three Danas admired the window displays of beautiful Thai silk in brilliant colors.

"I understand," said Aunt Harriet, "that originally only members of the aristocracy wore clothing made from these beautiful materials. An American army officer stationed here decided to introduce the silks to other countries. After a few years he did this, and now the fabrics are shipped to nearly every port in the world."

By this time the sightseers had reached a shop which sold nielloware—polished silver with a black design engraved in it. Jean heaved an admiring sigh. "Every bowl and plate and dish in this window is fascinating," she said. "I'd like to take them all home!"

Louise had walked on to the next shop where beautiful jewelry was displayed. As her aunt and sister caught up to her, she cried out, "Did you ever see anything so beautiful? Look at those rubies and those star sapphires!"

Aunt Harriet laughed. "Window shopping in Bangkok, I can see, is going to be quite a temptation! We will have to buy lots of souvenirs before we leave."

The Danas were fascinated by the adults and children walking along the street. Most of them were round-faced and smiling. They had straight black hair and snapping dark eyes.

"I feel like hugging every child I see!" Louise murmured.

When the Danas returned to the Oriental Hotel, the room clerk introduced them to a police officer who was waiting. The group walked over to the central part of the lobby where there was an attractive indoor garden. Louise acted as spokesman and asked the officer if a man named Swad Holden had entered Bangkok.

"No, he has not," the officer replied. "Will you please tell me why you are interested."

Louise related the full story of the stolen bamboo bird which belonged to Malee Wongsuwan. "We heard in Tokyo that Swad Holden was heading for Bangkok."

"All planes have been checked," the officer said.

"Perhaps he is here under an assumed name," Jean suggested.

"Possibly," the officer said. He frowned. "It is strange, though, how anyone could leave Tokyo under one name and arrive here under another. Our immigration officials are very efficient."

Louise assured the man that she did not doubt this. But she suggested that if Holden had stolen the Garuda, he probably was very clever in all sorts of devious ways.

"We shall make every effort to find this man," the officer promised. "Have you any idea why he might have come to Bangkok?"

"No, I don't," Louise replied, "but I suspect that his presence means trouble."

The officer thanked the Danas for their information, then stood up, bowed, and left. The Danas went to their rooms and Louise and Jean discussed this latest angle of the case. Was Holden in Bangkok or wasn't he?

"I'm inclined to think," said Jean, "that not only did Holden use another name, but he probably has passports from various countries under assumed names which he got with fake birth certificates.

"Perhaps," Louise agreed, "but also, he may have

planted the story in Tokyo about a trip to Bangkok just to throw the authorities off the track."

Just then the telephone rang and Louise answered it. Malee was calling. "I must talk fast," she said. "First, my mother wishes you to come to dinner this evening."

After Louise had accepted for the group, Malee went on, "Please do not say anything about the theft of my Garuda bird tonight. My parents and I hope you girls will have a wonderful time while you are staying in our country. I want to thank you both very much for all your help. But I will not need it any more."

"You mean your mystery is solved?" Louise exclaimed.

"No, but—" There was a pause, then Malee said, "I cannot talk further. I will see you at dinner."

## CHAPTER XII

# River Ceremony

When Louise told Jean of Malee's request, the girls sat staring at each other, stunned. Malee wanted them to give up the mystery!

"I call that downright ungrateful!" Jean stormed. "Here we've come halfway around the world to do that very thing and we're called off the case!"

Louise looked at her sister a little disapprovingly. "There's something you've forgotten, Jean," she said. "Malee's parents have paid for our transportation to and from Bangkok and offered to entertain us in their home. It was Aunt Harriet who wanted to come to the hotel and pay our expenses here."

Jean was not to be calmed easily. "That's all true," she conceded. "But Swad Holden *is* an international suspect wanted by the police. Our clues are pretty definite that he's the one who took the bamboo bird and the golden Buddha which Malee wants returned. Why should we stop hunting for him?"

At that moment Aunt Harriet came into the room. After hearing about the dinner invitation and Malee's request, she said, "It's my guess that when Malee divulged her suspicion to her parents they insisted that the search be stopped. To have you girls do anything more about trying to solve the theft may embarrass the Wongsuwan family."

Jean walked around the room several times, looked out the window at the river traffic, then sat down. "I'm not giving up yet," she stated, "but I promise to follow Malee's wishes, and say nothing about the mystery tonight. Who knows? We might even pick up a good clue at the Wongsuwans' home."

Aunt Harriet smiled. "My advice to you is just to have a good time tonight. Keep your eyes open if you like, but don't play detective!" she admonished.

Jean subsided and finally agreed to follow the suggestion. The three Danas dressed in the simple, attractive clothes which their room boy had pressed perfectly. As the group came down into the lobby later, they were met by Nai Samret. He bowed and said the car was at the door.

Half an hour later they arrived at the estate where Malee lived. The drive leading up to the rambling, two-story house, built of native wood, was bordered by coconut and pandanus palms and banana trees. There were clumps of bushes with white and pink camellias in full bloom. In a corner of the large lawn stood a group of stately bamboo trees, and, by itself, a lovely teak.

The chauffeur pulled up to the main entrance. At once Malee and her sister Pratoom came out to greet the visitors, with Boonmi directly behind them. The Danas were led inside and taken to a large loggia furnished with comfortable bamboo chairs and sofas. In the center of the open-sided room the girls noticed a large glass table. Upon closer inspection they saw that the center was concave, forming a huge flower bowl. In it floated pinkish-lavender flowers.

"These are lotus blossoms," Malee explained.

Mr. and Mrs. Wongsuwan appeared, and shortly after, a gong sounded, summoning everyone to dinner. Malee explained that her uncle was out of town and her great-aunt in bed, since she was not feeling well.

"What a beautiful dining room!" Louise thought, as she noted the finely carved, teakwood furniture and the tan Thai silk draperies.

The Danas were very careful not to make any reference to the mystery. Malee, who had seemed nervous at first, now relaxed, and conversation was confined almost entirely to customs in Thailand and to school life at Starhurst.

Deft servants served a first course of delicious native fish. Then came chicken, followed by bowls of rice and an assortment of curries. For dessert there was a variety of native fruits. The Danas selected mangosteens, which were about the size of a small apple and deep purple in color. The fruit inside was pure white and very sweet.

When dinner was over, Malee offered to show the Danas through the house.

Everywhere the furniture was upholstered with beautiful Thai silk and on the walls hung cloth scrolls with designs of ancient life in Siam. Louise and Jean giggled over one scene which showed the master of a house and his wife presumably having a private conversation on the porch of their home. Swinging in the hammock hung high in a tree nearby was an eavesdropping servant!

"How amusing." Aunt Harriet chuckled.

On the second floor the girls were particularly fascinated by the beds which stood only a few inches above the floor. They were of wood, and several of the large headboards were painted with gay flowers or river scenes.

Louise and Jean had noticed that from the start of their tour Boonmi had kept right behind them. In back of him was another man, apparently a servant, who seemed to be listening attentively to every word that was being said. Twice Boonmi spoke sharply to him, and although the girls could not understand what he was saying, they felt that he was giving some order which the servant evidently was not obeying.

When the group came downstairs they gathered again on the loggia. Suddenly Louise noticed that

Aunt Harriet had a strange look on her face. Following the direction of her aunt's eyes, Louise saw a tiny lizard scurrying across the floor. She suppressed a giggle.

"I should like to show you my cats," Malee spoke up. "I will get them." She went into the house and returned in a few moments carrying a Siamese cat under each arm.

She put them on the floor in front of Louise and Jean who were seated on a sofa. At once the tawny-and-black, smooth-haired cats gave low guttural growls which sounded more like those of a dog than a cat. Jean bent over to pat the animals, but they backed away and continued to growl.

"I'm afraid they're not very friendly with strangers," said Malee, "but they are wonderful watchdogs."

Louise smiled. "They're very beautiful, anyway."

"Shall we walk out into the garden with the cats?" Malee proposed.

Instantly Louise and Jean stood up and followed their school friend. They had a feeling that she wished to talk to them privately and explain more fully what she had been unable to tell them over the telephone. But if Malee had this in mind, she had no opportunity to talk because Boonmi joined them at once. It seemed to the Danas that his presence made Malee very uncomfortable, but she did not comment.

She led the girls to the teak tree. "The gathering of teak is the largest industry in Thailand after rice," Malee explained. "The forests are up in the northern part where it's cooler. I hope we can make a trip to the teak country. It is interesting to watch the elephants at work rolling the logs down to the rivers."

All this time Boonmi had said nothing. He continued to eye the Dana girls as if he were trying to learn something from their conversation. Louise and Jean were annoyed. Did Malee's secret about her family have something to do with her brother-in-law? Perhaps he was the one who was responsible for having Malee ask the Danas not to work on the mystery any longer!

They all went back to the loggia and in a little while Pratoom said, "Tonight there will be an interesting ceremony on the river. It is called a Loy Krathong. We attend it as the moon is rising."

"We'd love to go," Louise replied.

Before they left, Aunt Harriet presented Mrs. Wongsuwan with the gift of place mats and napkins which she had brought. As was the custom, Malee's mother did not open the package, but bowed low and expressed her gratitude to the Danas for their very kind remembrance. Since she and Mr. Wongsuwan were not going to the Loy Krathong, the Danas thanked them for a delightful evening.

"We trust you will be our guests in the United States some time," Aunt Harriet said.

Just as the young people were going toward the drive, where the chauffeur awaited them in the car, the servant who had followed Boonmi before, now appeared and spoke to him. Malee whispered to the girls, "That's Thongchai, my brother-in-law's personal servant."

A moment later Thongchai hurried off. Boonmi, Pratoom, Malee, and the Danas stepped into the car and were driven to the east bank of the Menam Chao Phraya River. Here an enchanting sight met their eyes! Hundreds of people lined the shores and tiny lights danced on the water. Malee explained that miniature boats, each equipped with a lighted candle, and some with incense and a handful of ticals, were sent out from the shore.

"Originally these little boats were made from leaves shaped like a cup. They are set adrift to bring us luck. But nowadays the containers are made of wood or even plastic and are in the shape of boats or birds.

"I have brought one for each of us," Malee went on. "Would you like to launch some boats?"

The three Danas thought this would be great fun. Jean laughingly said, "Who couldn't use a little luck?"

After their six boats had been sent off, Malee and her sister began to sing a song. It was very lilting and sounded like a lullaby.

At the finish Pratoom said, "The little song is directed to our boats and is asking them to bring us good fortune. We must watch our boats until they are out of sight."

The girls peered ahead, but with so many floating candles on the river, it was soon difficult to distinguish their own. The swift-flowing water carried the little boats away at a rapid pace.

Suddenly the Danas heard the rush of feet behind them. Before they could turn to see who the oncoming persons were, two youths grabbed Louise and Jean and pushed them into the water. All four went down out of sight.

Aunt Harriet gave a startled gasp, then said indignantly, "I don't think this is very funny. Is it part of the celebration?"

"N-no!" Malee replied, puzzled and embarrassed.

The group on shore waited for the sisters and their assailants to reappear. But precious seconds went by. They did not rise to the surface!

CHAPTER XIII

# The Lurking Figure

"SOMETHING has happened to Louise and Jean!" Aunt Harriet cried out in terror. She looked around for Boonmi, expecting him to jump to the rescue and help the submerged girls. But he was nowhere in sight!

"I'll go after them!" Malee exclaimed.

But as she ran forward, Nai Samret cried out, "I saw what happened. I will go." The chauffeur dived in.

Meanwhile, Louise and Jean were having an under-water battle with their assailants. It became apparent that the two men who had pushed the sisters into the water were determined to keep them below the surface.

Louise and Jean were excellent swimmers and could hold their breath for a long time. But presently the girls realized that they must have air soon. Their lungs felt ready to burst!

Suddenly they saw a third man swimming under-water toward them. Desperately they hoped he was coming to their rescue!

Their two assailants also saw him. Instantly they shoved the girls with tremendous force toward the bottom of the river. Then the men rose to the surface and swam off quickly, evidently frightened away by the newcomer.

Louise and Jean swam to the surface and took in deep drafts of fresh air. They did not try to make shore. Instead, they lay on their backs, motionless and breathing deeply.

Finally Louise said, "You okay, sis?"

"Yes. And you?"

"All right."

Nai Samret helped them climb up onto the bank and Aunt Harriet clasped the girls in her arms.

"Those dreadful men!" she cried out. "What were they trying to do—drown you?"

Louise and Jean had a strong hunch that was exactly what the men had had in mind, but they did not want to worry their aunt and merely laughed off the incident.

Jean said lightly, "Maybe getting dunked at the Loy Krathong is a Thai custom."

Malee and Pratoom had been greatly upset. Now Pratoom spoke up indignantly. "It is not, believe me!" and Malee added, "This is not a day to be desecrated. It has a religious significance."

The Danas, meanwhile, had looked for their assailants. There was no sign of them. Boonmi, too, seemed to have disappeared, and Pratoom and Malee gave no explanation for his absence.

Louise and Jean thanked the chauffeur again, then Aunt Harriet said they must leave.

"Yes." Jean grinned. "Louise and I must be a sight in these wet clothes! And thanks so much for bringing us to the river celebration."

Nai Samret quickly took plastic raincoats from the trunk of the car and wrapped them around the dripping girls. He then drove the Danas to the hotel. When the sisters, with their aunt, stepped into the elevator, the boy who was running it eyed them curiously. But he was too polite to ask what had happened to the bedraggled girls. They in turn gave no explanation, merely saying good night when they reached their floor.

Aunt Harriet came into her nieces' room as they were preparing for bed. "Have you any explanation for what happened?" she asked.

Determined not to worry her, and not having proof of their suspicions anyway, Louise and Jean said only that they were puzzled.

By morning the sisters felt completely refreshed, despite the harrowing experience of the previous night. One thing which still bothered them was why Boonmi had disappeared.

"Let's go down to the riverbank and see if we can pick up any kind of a clue," Louise suggested. "We'll have plenty of time before breakfast. I'll write a note and stick it under Aunt Harriet's door."

Louise and Jean dressed and walked quickly to the spot where they had launched their boats the previous evening. The muddy area was covered with footprints going in every direction.

"I'm afraid these mean nothing," Louise remarked. "Well, I guess we'll have to give up—" She suddenly stopped and exclaimed, "Here's something!" She held up a half-smoked cigarette. "It's a Weathervane!"

"Swad Holden's brand!" Jean cried out. "Do you suppose *he* was here last evening, spying on us?"

"It could be." Louise nodded. "One of the men that shoved us into the water might even have been Holden!"

"I had the impression that those men who pushed us were more slender than Swad Holden's supposed to be," Jean stated. "But I'm beginning to be rather suspicious of Boonmi. I don't like the way he follows Malee around when we're with her, never giving us a chance to be alone. Who knows—if he *is* up to something, he might have asked those two men to push us into the water."

"The cigarette may be a valuable clue, anyhow," Louise said.

The sisters walked thoughtfully back to the Oriental Hotel and reached their room just as Aunt Harriet was coming out of hers. She kissed them both, then said, "Well, did my detectives pick up any clues?"

"Perhaps," Jean answered. "Aunt Harriet, what do you think of Boonmi?"

Miss Dana pursed her lips. "He doesn't seem very friendly, but if you are implying that he is not aboveboard, what proof have you?"

Louise laughed. "None, Aunt Harriet, but we *are* suspicious of him because he seems to be trying to keep Malee from talking to us."

"It does seem so from the way he acts," Aunt Harriet agreed. "Well, shall we go down and have some breakfast? There's a lovely outdoor restaurant."

The Danas thoroughly enjoyed the dining room along the river. While they were eating, a phone call came for Louise from Malee.

"How are you and Jean feeling?" she inquired.

"Oh, we're fine, thank you."

"Then we should like very much to take you to the palace grounds this morning," Malee said.

"We'd love to go," Louise replied.

Then, on impulse, she decided to find out what kind of cigarettes Boonmi smoked, if any. Deftly she led the conversation to the subject of mementos and souvenirs which the Danas wanted to take back to the States.

"My Uncle Ned smokes," Louise went on. "I've heard that Thai cigarettes are very good." She laughed. "But I suppose one can't top English brands. What does your brother-in-law smoke?"

"I really do not know," Malee said. "I will find out. Someone gives them to him." She left the telephone and in a few minutes returned to say, "Boonmi smokes Weathervanes."

Louise's pulses quickened. She had not noticed Boonmi smoking. By some chance had Holden been there? And was he the "someone" who gave Boonmi the Weathervanes?

"Will you be ready in an hour?" Malee asked.

"That'll be fine." Louise said good-by, then went back to the table to tell her sister and aunt about the trip.

When the Danas were ready to leave, Louise picked up her camera. "I hope Boonmi won't be tagging along," she remarked to Jean. "I'd like to have a talk alone with Malee."

To the sisters' disappointment, the Thai girl's brother-in-law was waiting for them in the lobby with Pratoom and Malee. After saying good morning, Boonmi remarked how sorry he was that he had not been with the group when the girls had been shoved into the water.

"I saw some friends of mine at a distance and stayed to talk with them," he said.

Abruptly changing the subject, Boonmi told the Danas that the palace was no longer used as a residence, but that the temples on the grounds were most interesting.

The Wongsuwans' chauffeur drove the group to

the palace gate. Malee asked him to return for the sightseers in an hour, and they got out.

As the Danas walked over a bridge across a klong and through the entrance gate to the spacious grounds, the dazzling beauty of the shimmering temples left them breathless. Some of the exquisite buildings were big, some small, many had curving, three-tiered roofs which ended at the lower corners in slender upsweeping, serpentlike bodies.

There were no other sightseers around then and Jean and Louise relaxed in the peaceful atmosphere. At every turn there was Oriental splendor, and the Danas admired the statues, the endless gilded porticoes, and the graceful columns.

They passed several chedies on their walk, and exclaimed at the sight of the towering half-god, half-animal statues of grotesque-looking monsters that watched over the entrance to the temples.

"Fascinating!" Louise whispered to her sister. But Jean, at that moment, was glancing back over her shoulder for another look at the beautiful mosaic work on a tomb.

Suddenly she was startled to see a man peering from behind one of the monster statues and beckoning toward someone in their group. He had all the physical characteristics of her mental image of Swad Holden!

Before she had a chance to tell Louise, Boonmi said, "Walk straight ahead and wait for me at the Temple of the Emerald Buddha."

A man peered from behind a statue and beckoned to someone.

Malee and Pratoom complied. They walked on with Aunt Harriet without turning around. Jean, however, rushed over and grabbed her sister's arm. Quickly she whispered what she had seen.

Amazed, Louise whispered back, "Do you think Swad Holden was signaling Boonmi?"

Jean nodded. "I'll bet Boonmi's gone to meet him! Let's run around this other building and come up to that chedi from the rear. If I can snap a picture of Holden, we can give it to the police."

Jean and Louise had no time to excuse themselves from their aunt and the Thai girls, who now were some distance ahead. They darted around a corner where they hoped to get a better view of the two men without being seen.

Unfortunately, they found their way blocked off by other buildings. They started back toward the chedi by another route, but by this time Boonmi was returning. He looked annoyed when he saw the girls and icily asked what they had been doing, and why they were not at the temple.

Jean replied nonchalantly, "I wanted to take a certain picture."

Ignoring Boonmi, she walked toward the chedi, took a snapshot of the building, then quickly scanned the ground for a possible clue to the man who had been hiding there. She saw a partly smoked Weathervane cigarette!

Louise had hesitated to follow Jean for fear of drawing attention to their actions. Jean was aware of this and called Louise to come quickly—that she had just seen something very intriguing.

As soon as Louise reached her sister's side, Jean showed her the cigarette, then led her to the street. But the man was not in sight.

"I'm sure he was Holden," Jean said. "Louise, do you think this meeting proves that Swad Holden and Boonmi are friends?"

"It certainly looks like it. But we'd better not say anything yet." After a moment's pause, Louise remarked thoughtfully, "Maybe Malee's secret worry is that she knows the two men are friends!"

CHAPTER XIV

# The Rescue

LOUISE and Jean hurried back to their group and caught up to them at the Temple of the Emerald Buddha.

"This is called the Wat Phra Keo," she explained. "We must remove our shoes before entering. It is a custom we follow in our temples."

She explained that the statue of the Emerald Buddha was not very large, only two feet high, but very precious to the Thai people.

"It is the only statue of the teacher whose garments are draped according to the seasons," she said. "This Buddha is so sacred that only the king is allowed to climb the little ladder behind the altar and make the change of clothing."

The Danas and their friends removed their shoes and walked into the beautiful Wat Phra Keo. A gathering of worshipers were seated on the floor, most of them oblivious of one another and of the newcomers. Some looked down as if praying, others lifted their eyes toward the ceiling. A few turned and smiled at the Danas. Jean and Louise recalled what Malee had said about Buddhists—they sought enlightenment and endeavored to practice tolerance in their daily lives.

The altar was some distance ahead of the visitors. It was built in tiers and appeared to be of pure gold. There were statues representing Buddha in various kindly moods.

At the very top of the altar, not far below the ceiling, was a seated statue of Buddha. It was entirely green, and Malee whispered it was made of jade.

"The statue is very old, and, it is said, has traveled farther than any other," Malee explained. "The story is that the Emerald Buddha was carved in India, taken to China, from there to Burma, Ceylon, and finally brought here."

The Buddha's scarflike garment, she pointed out, belonged to the rainy season. It lay over his left shoulder and entirely covered the rest of the figure. On the statue's head was a tight-fitting, spiral-shaped cap which reached down over the ears and looked like gold. According to Malee, the seasonal garment would be changed any day.

"This is the temple in which the king worships," Pratoom added.

As the sightseers tiptoed from the building and once more put on their shoes, Louise asked Malee and her sister about a young man who was standing nearby. He was swathed in a saffron-colored robe. The girls had seen many similarly robed figures on the streets. The men wore their hair cut very short. Some were barefoot, while others wore sandals.

"They are serving in the Buddhist priesthood for three months or more," Malee explained. "Every man in Thailand must enter for this length of time. Some of them remain priests for the rest of their lives."

"During the time they are in training, these young men learn real humility," Pratoom pointed out. "They must live in monasteries and study a great deal. No food is served to them there. They carry bowls on their walks and trust kindhearted people to give them rice or fish or fruit."

"While the bowls are being filled," Malee added, "the young priests keep their heads turned and then walk away. It is part of the custom that they do not thank the donors. We consider it a great privilege to offer food to the priests who have no money during the period they are in the priesthood."

"How truly inspiring!" Aunt Harriet remarked.

Boonmi reminded the others that the hour of sightseeing was up. The Danas regretted having to leave but went outside the palace grounds where Nai Samret waited with the car.

Pratoom suggested that the Americans might like to visit a factory where Thai silk was made. "One place handles the whole process from the cocoon of the silkworm through to the finished bolt of cloth," she said. "Shall we go there?"

Aunt Harriet and her nieces accepted this suggestion eagerly. As they started off, Louise and Jean felt that Boonmi might leave them shortly. Surely he must have some kind of work to do! Furthermore, he was too austere to be interested in dress materials! But to their annoyance Boonmi went along.

The chauffeur finally stopped at a somewhat muddy road which bordered a narrow klong. He apologized for not being able to take the sightseers all the way into the factory, which bordered the waterfront, but he was afraid the heavy car would get stuck.

The passengers got out and carefully made their way forward. In the klong, children were swimming and laughing and playing games. It seemed as if even the youngest could keep afloat!

"They seem to love it," Louise remarked to Jean.

As the sisters watched the scene along the klong, they saw a naked baby girl not much over a year old toddle from a house across the way and walk toward the dock.

"Oh!" the two girls cried out.

The infant fell headlong into the water! There was hardly a ripple and none of the children around had noticed the accident.

With long strides the Danas were at the water's edge. They jumped into a moored boat and Jean paddled furiously across the narrow expanse of the klong.

By the time the baby had risen to the surface, the Danas were at her side. Louise reached out and pulled the little body into the boat. Together the girls gave the choking tot first aid and soon she began to cry.

The native swimmers crowded around as the child's mother ran from the house. She took her tiny daughter and clasped the child lovingly. In English she said:

"Thank you. Sorry." Apparently this was the extent of her knowledge of English.

Louise and Jean smiled, bowed, and paddled back to their waiting friends. Malee, Pratoom, and Aunt Harriet praised the girls for saving the baby's life. "You have endeared yourselves to everyone here," Malee said.

Boonmi made no comment. Louise and Jean paid no attention to this, however, and followed the others to the Thai silk factory.

The one-story building had walls on only three sides. The fourth was open to the klong. On the open side, a man was working busily under the shade of a large banyan tree. Malee explained that he was forming hanks of raw silk, which previously had been wound onto reels from the silkworm cocoons. These hanks would then be boiled to remove the gummy substance which covered the silk threads.

Nearby was a round stone fireplace with a pit in the middle, over which hung a caldron on a tripod. Pratoom pointed out that the thread was being dyed here. Next it would be washed, then hung up to dry. Finally it would be spun once more onto huge spools to be used in the looms.

"Come inside and we'll show you the weavers," Malee suggested, leading the way.

The Danas followed her down one aisle and up another. Smiling, barefoot young women sat on wide benches before the looms, which were large and intricately threaded with long strands of vari-colored silk. With amazing speed the weavers' feet pushed first one treadle, then another. As various strands of silk were lifted, the workers' deft fingers threw the shuttle from side to side among the many long threads.

Most of the silks were a combination of two colors and gave the finished material a shimmering quality.

"They are simply exquisite!" Jean burst out. "The materials must be frightfully expensive."

Pratoom smiled. "They do not cost so much in our country, but I understand that in the United States one would have to pay six or seven times as much for them."

"Would it be possible to buy a few yards here?" Aunt Harriet inquired.

"Not here," Pratoom answered, "but there is a shop near your hotel which sells the product of this factory. If you like, we can stop there on our way back."

"I'd like to make a few purchases, and I'm sure Louise and Jean would," Aunt Harriet said.

Louise nodded. She was thinking, "Certainly Boonmi won't follow us into the silk shop and Jean and I can talk with Malee alone."

But once more this proved to be a false hope. Not only did Boonmi follow Aunt Harriet and the girls into the shop, but he stayed very close to them every minute.

The Danas learned that the store sold not only Thai silk by the yard, but also fascinating handbags, neckties, and scarves.

"Here's a scarf like the one Mrs. Randolph wore in Penfield!" Jean exclaimed.

The Danas selected several ties and scarves for relatives and friends, and Aunt Harriet bought a number of dress lengths of silk.

When their shopping was finished, the Danas were driven to the hotel. Although they cordially invited the others to come inside, Boonmi said that he, Malee, and Pratoom must hurry home. The Americans thanked them for the wonderful morning and said good-by.

"I will phone you about more sightseeing plans," Malee called, as the car pulled away.

"Boonmi is certainly acting suspiciously," Jean burst out. "I wish I knew the reason."

Louise nodded, then suggested that the Danas

do some sightseeing that afternoon by themselves. Aunt Harriet smilingly confessed that she was a bit weary, and that she would like to rest after lunch.

"You don't mind if we go out by ourselves?" Jean asked her.

"Of course not," her aunt replied. With a twinkle, she added, "Something tells me you'll also do a little sleuthing."

Jean and Louise laughed, then told their aunt the full story about the man who had been hiding by the chedi in the palace grounds.

"I'm sure, from the glimpse I had of him, he is Swad Holden," Jean declared. "I'd like to walk around Bangkok and look for him. Perhaps we'll be lucky and spot him somewhere. We might even take a boat ride."

"It sounds like hunting for a needle in a haystack," Aunt Harriet remarked, "but I have no objection to your trying."

Lunch over, the girls walked along the various city thoroughfares toward the waterfront.

"Let's see if we can rent a sampan," Louise suggested.

One was waiting at a nearby dock and she asked the boatman to take them for a ride. Unfortunately, he did not speak English. They continued to the next dock, where another sampan was tied up. Through gestures the sisters finally made the smiling boatman understand what they wanted, and he agreed.

"Listen!" Jean said suddenly as the girls were about to get into the boat. "I thought I heard someone calling our names."

A moment later both sisters distinctly heard, "Louise! Jean!"

They turned and saw Malee Wongsuwan running toward them at top speed. To their surprise, she wore a light coat, though it was very warm. In one hand she was holding a typical high-peaked Thai hat. Its tiers were made of gold and bits of colored glass, and there was a strap to go under the chin.

"I had a hard time finding you," she said breathlessly. "Your aunt thought you might go for a boat ride, so I came down here."

The Danas were curious as to how Malee happened to be alone, but made no comment.

Malee continued, "I *must* talk to you girls. By the way, I brought along this hat and a costume as souvenirs for you."

She removed her coat and showed them a satin trouser-and-jacket suit decorated with gold braid.

"How stunning!" Louise exclaimed. "You mean we can take this home?"

"Yes," Malee replied. "Would you like it?"

"Indeed we would," Jean answered. "Aren't you sweet! It's beautiful."

She asked Malee to put on the hat so that they would know exactly how to adjust it. When the headpiece was in place, the Danas thought they had never seen anyone look prettier than the dark-haired Thai girl did at that moment.

Louise, whose eyes had wandered past Malee toward the river, caught sight of a small dugout-type canoe. A boy of about twelve was poling it along near the shore.

"Look what's on the seat of that boat!" Louise cried out excitedly.

The boy seemed to know what Louise had said. Instantly he picked up the object and held it aloft.

*It was a golden bamboo Garuda bird exactly like the one that had been stolen from Malee!*

CHAPTER XV

# A Hunch Comes True

THE three girls stood thunderstruck at sight of the decorated bamboo Garuda bird held up by the young boy. As he laid it back on the boat seat and began to pole away, Louise cried out:

"Oh, don't go! We want to talk to you!"

A frightened look came over the lad's face, but quickly Malee spoke to him in Thai. Then she translated for the girls. "I was telling him he has nothing to worry about."

At her request he pulled close to shore and let the girls examine the bird. Malee recognized a few slight differences from the one she had owned, but said it was almost a duplicate. She opened the little door and looked inside. There was nothing within.

"Ask the boy where this came from," Jean urged.

There was a short conversation in Thai between Malee and the youngster. Then she told the sisters that the bird had come from the home of people named Chamnan. Several of the birds were being made on the order of a fine Thai gentleman. "The boy does not know the man's name."

At Louise's suggestion, Malee asked the boy to take the girls to the house where the bamboo birds were being made. The youngster hedged and admitted he should not have taken the bird.

"He is afraid the Chamnans will be angry," Malee reported. "He tells me he only borrowed the bird, and was on his way to return it."

Malee and the Danas conferred, then Malee said to the boy with a disarming smile, "We won't tell that you borrowed the bird. We'd just like to see where it was made."

"You get boat and come with me," he agreed.

The Danas told Malee that they had planned to rent the sampan which was waiting. The three girls climbed aboard, and directed their boatman to follow the boy. He nodded and began poling the dugout up the river.

Soon the youngster turned into a klong. The sampan was close behind. Finally both craft turned into a bisecting canal.

The boy covered the bird with a sarong which was lying in his boat. Presently he drew up before a thatched-roof house set on poles, and stepped out onto the dock. He did not go into the front of the house, but walked around to the back. The girls surmised that he hoped to return the bird surreptitiously.

The Danas did not ask their boatman to stop poling at this point. They waited until he had proceeded some distance up the klong. Then Louise requested him to turn around and start back. As they approached the house into which the boy had gone, a woman stood in front of it, waist-deep in water, bathing her baby boy.

"Isn't he cunning?" Louise said. "Let's stop."

As the boatman drew up, Malee asked the woman if she spoke English and she nodded.

"My friends are from the United States," Malee said. "We were admiring your lovely baby."

"He's a darling," Louise spoke up. "What is your son's name?"

"We just call him Little One," the woman answered, and the Danas wondered how they might learn more without seeming to be inquisitive.

"Do you have other children?" Jean inquired.

"No."

Louise decided to try one more approach. "You have a large, attractive house. Does your husband work at home?"

The child's mother scowled. "No, he works in a nielloware factory."

The Danas realized they were not making much progress in pursuing the clue of the bamboo birdmakers. Both girls, nonetheless, felt that there was a tie-in between Malee's bird and the one the boy had borrowed.

Suddenly Louise had an idea. "We have been sightseeing around Bangkok but haven't had the good fortune to visit any of your homes along a klong," she said courteously to the baby's mother.

The woman's eyes flashed and she spoke rapidly in Thai to Malee. When translated, the reply was, "I am very busy and do not want them to come inside. I wish you would leave."

The Danas reddened. They had found the Thai people so friendly and co-operative that the woman's rebuff rather startled them. The girls apologized for having bothered her and directed their boatman to pole off.

As they proceeded down the klong, Malee drew the Danas toward her and whispered, "My brother-in-law has been acting very strangely ever since I arrived home. He is trying to get my father to send me and you girls right back to the States. And he will not let me out of his sight, as you have doubtless noticed."

Malee paused and took a deep breath. "Louise and Jean, I am wondering if Boonmi is carrying on some kind of dishonest dealing, and is afraid you detectives will learn what it is. I have spoken to my father about this. He hopes it isn't true, of course, but is not sure what to think."

"What do you base your suspicions on?" Louise asked, with a meaningful glance at Jean. So they had been right about Malee's secret!

The Thai girl was silent for several seconds before she replied, "While I was at Starhurst, Pratoom wrote me a couple of letters. As you Americans say,

I could read between the lines that she was not happy. Certain things had happened which made her feel that her husband might be involved in some unethical financial dealings."

"And this was the secret which you didn't want to tell us?" Louise inquired gently.

"Yes. I did not think so much about it until after my bamboo bird was stolen," Malee answered. "But you can understand now why I fear some international complications. With my father prominent in Thailand, and my cousin working in the Embassy, any scandal would be most embarrassing."

"Indeed it would," Jean agreed.

"What do you girls think?" their school friend asked, looking at them intently.

Jean blurted out, "I'm sorry, but I must admit we've been suspicious of your brother-in-law. You didn't know this, but today when we were on the palace grounds, I saw a man hiding behind a chedi who I am sure was Swad Holden. He was beckoning to Boonmi—who did leave us abruptly, you recall."

"Oh, dear," Malee said worriedly.

"Everything will work out," Louise said soothingly to the distraught girl. "Why don't you tell your father about this morning's episode?"

"I will do that," the Thai girl promised. Then she sighed. "If there should be a scandal concerning Boonmi, it will be dreadful for my sister.

She adores her husband and we have always thought he was a fine man. He is an engineer at our gold mine. Pratoom believes that unwittingly he has become implicated in an unscrupulous scheme."

Both Dana girls admitted that the situation was a delicate one and advised Malee to proceed with great caution.

"I will," Malee assured them. "And do not tell Boonmi I was with you this afternoon."

The Danas agreed. They spoke of the Chamnans' house on the klong, and tried to think of some way to learn more about it.

"You mean perhaps Boonmi is mixed up with making the bamboo birds?" Malee asked.

"Possibly," Jean answered.

Malee was thoughtful, then she said, "Maybe we can find out. My father has two motorboats. Boonmi often goes away in one of them. Perhaps I can persuade my father to follow him. If so, the next time Boonmi goes out in the boat I will phone you."

When they reached the boatman's dock, Louise paid him, then the girls went to the sisters' room in the Oriental Hotel. Malee took off the costume under which she wore a light silk suit. Before leaving, she extended an invitation to all the Danas to attend the classical dances that evening with her and Pratoom and Boonmi.

"I hope you will enjoy the performance," she said. "Be sure to watch the dancers' hands."

The Danas accepted with pleasure, then Malee said good-by. That evening the Wongsuwans drove the group to the dance performance.

"Before we reach the theater," Malee said as they rode along, "I should like to tell you something about the Thai classical drama. It is very, very old and is modeled on ancient Sanskrit. There is dialogue and chorus singing, as well as a special type of dancing. One must learn what the various movements mean—for instance, if the hand is put over the heart, it indicates love. If one stamps the feet hard and points at someone with a forefinger, it means one is angry."

Pratoom explained that these gestures had to be very pronounced because the actors' faces were usually covered by masks.

Once inside the well-filled auditorium, the group took seats and presently the actors came onstage. The Danas had never seen so much glitter. Both men and women were attired in costumes of brocaded satin ornamented with jewels and gold-and-silver trimming.

The women had on ankle-length, close-fitting skirts. A panel of highly decorated material reached from the back of the neck to the heels. The dancers' wavy black hair was shoulder length, and they wore the traditional tapering jeweled hats.

The men's costumes consisted of snug breeches and a bodice of silver with gold cord crisscrossing the back and front and ending in hip ornaments.

Three small jeweled panels hung from the waist.

Both the men and women dancers had bracelets on their arms and ankles. They wore slippers with toes that curved up and backward, matching the position of their hands.

"Aren't the gestures intriguing?" Louise whispered to Jean. "The dancers can bend their fingers backward almost double!"

Malee overheard the remark and whispered, "Dancers have to start early in their childhood to learn to do that. It is impossible later on."

The performers' heavily powdered and rouged faces, together with the exaggerated heavy black eyebrows and ruby-red lips, gave them a very mask-like look. They moved rhythmically and gracefully in most exotic and intriguing patterns.

Louise turned to Malee and asked, "Do the men always dance with their knees bent to the side?"

"Yes," Malee replied. "It is a Thai custom."

"Everything seems to go perfectly with the music," Louise remarked. "And it sounds so different from what we're used to."

Malee smiled. "Yes, it does, but after you hear it awhile, I believe you will find the five-tone scale fascinating and satisfying."

The performance was very long, and it seemed to the Danas that with each number the costumes became more exquisite, and the dancing steps more intricate. When the show was over, Louise and Jean were starry-eyed in admiration.

"We've never seen anything more beautiful," Louise declared.

Malee and Pratoom expressed their delight also, but Boonmi did not say a word. On several occasions during the performance Louise and Jean had caught him staring at them as if he were trying to read their minds. At times it made the sisters very uncomfortable, but they tried to act unconcerned.

They in turn had watched him closely, hoping to detect some expression which might be a clue to his thoughts. His face remained impassive.

When the three Danas reached their hotel rooms, they undressed and tumbled into bed quickly. All of them were very weary and ready for a sound night's sleep.

It seemed to Louise and Jean that they had been asleep only a short time when the telephone rang. Opening their eyes, the sisters realized it was morning, but it was extremely early. Who could be calling?

Jean reached from her bed, took the receiver, and said, "Hello."

"Jean?" It was Malee's voice and she sounded excited. "Boonmi left the house a few minutes ago with Thongchai. My father knows where they will stop for gasoline, so we can trail him from there. Shall we pick you up at the Oriental Hotel dock in a little while?"

"Oh, yes!" said Jean, now thoroughly awake.

"We'll dress immediately and meet you there in a few minutes."

Louise was already out of bed and dashing into the bathroom to wash her face in cold water to wake herself up fully. The girls dressed quickly, then wrote a note which they thrust under Aunt Harriet's door, and hurried down the stairway to the lobby and out to the hotel dock.

Just as they arrived, Mr. Wongsuwan and Malee pulled up in the motorboat. The Danas jumped aboard and the sleuthing started!

## CHAPTER XVI

# The Chase in the Klong

THE chase after Boonmi and Thongchai led first along the Menam Chao Phraya River, then into the Klong Bang Luang. Louise and Jean learned that this particular canal was famous for its floating markets.

"Vegetables and fruits grown far up in the country are brought down here to Bangkok by boat," Malee explained.

Mr. Wongsuwan remarked that at this time of morning many natives came to make purchases and the water was apt to be full of boats. "We may find it hard to keep our quarry in sight," he stated.

About twenty minutes later his prediction came true. A real traffic jam developed on the klong!

"Oh, well," Louise said with a shrug, "if we're caught in this tie-up, so is Boonmi."

Malee's father said he would act as lookout, while Malee explained the sights to her friends. Some of the sampans had covered sections, inside of which bags of rice were piled high. Open boats carried a variety of fruits and vegetables. Most of the craft contained so much produce that there was scarcely room enough for the man or woman poling it.

"You didn't have time for breakfast," Malee remarked. "I shall buy some bananas for us. They are small, but you will find them delicious."

She bought a hand of them, and the hungry girls, as well as Mr. Wongsuwan, each ate four of the delectable fruit!

Suddenly Jean wrinkled her nose. "Phew! Something around here smells like overripe cheese. What in the world is it?"

Malee laughed softly. "Do you see that boat over there?" She pointed. "Those melons inside it are called durian."

She went on to explain that the outer shell of durian was prickly and gave off the offensive odor. But the pulp tasted delicious when scooped from the shell and left for a while in a cool place. "Like eating almonds mixed with sweet-scented rose petals," she concluded poetically.

Although the Wongsuwan motorboat was unable to make much progress at the moment, young children, deftly poling their small canoes through the maze of craft, glided by, smiling at the Americans.

"Everybody looks so happy," Louise remarked, "especially the children."

"They love this life on the klong," Malee told

her. She sighed. "There is talk that some day all the klongs will disappear and roads will take their place."

Her father turned a moment from his watching post in the bow of the craft to say, "When that happens, Bangkok will not be Bangkok. This klong life is what the people enjoy. I cannot imagine them living any other way. So long as they are healthy and happy, why should they change?"

He pointed out that illness per capita in Thailand was far below that of most countries in the Asian world.

Just then, traffic opened up and he guided the boat once more in pursuit of Boonmi and Thongchai. Suddenly he spied them and decided to keep at a safe distance, so that he would not be detected, but could see what the two men might be doing.

Presently Boonmi pulled up at a klong-side store, stopped, and got off. As Thongchai moved over to the pilot's seat, he called out loudly to his employer. Malee, who had been able to catch what he said, interpreted for the others. "I will come back and pick you up in a little while."

The sleuthing party was now in a quandary about what to do. Should they try to spy on Boonmi, or should they follow Thongchai?

Louise decided for them. "Maybe Thongchai is an accomplice in the underhanded scheme! Let's see where he's going!"

Mr. Wongsuwan agreed. "We must find out what his reason is for not waiting for Boonmi."

They continued to trail Boonmi's personal servant. A little while later Thongchai came to a large boat loaded to the water line with vegetables. Two young men were poling it.

Mr. Wongsuwan throttled down so that his boat was moving at a crawl. He and the girls took turns watching through binoculars he had brought along. The servant selected a few items, then pulled a handful of bills from a pocket and gave these to one of the men. He received no change, and quickly went off.

"Do vegetables cost *that* much?" Louise asked in a whisper.

"No," Mr. Wongsuwan replied. His eyes had narrowed and it was evident that he was very suspicious of the transaction.

He said nothing more, but the Danas guessed that Thongchai had paid far too much for his purchases, and that the extra money given to the men was for some other service. But what?

Conjectures raced through the sisters' minds. Was it possible that Boonmi, Thongchai, and Swad Holden were part of the same group working on some undercover scheme? Could it have anything to do with the people who were making the bamboo birds?

Jean whispered to Louise, "Maybe those two

vegetable vendors are the men who pushed us into the water! They're the same build. Perhaps they're just being paid for the job!"

At that point Thongchai began to turn his motorboat around. Mr. Wongsuwan quickly pulled his own craft out of sight into a bisecting klong. He went far enough up, so that he would not be detected. Then he swung about and re-entered the Klong Bang Luang. As he passed the two suspected vegetable men again, Louise took a picture of them without their being aware of it.

"This snapshot may come in handy as evidence," she told herself.

The Danas and Wongsuwans kept Thongchai in sight. Presently they saw him stop for Boonmi. The pair went swiftly down the klong toward the Menam Chao Phraya River. Malee and the Danas carried on a spirited conversation about what had happened.

"I am afraid, Louise and Jean, that you are disappointed so far in our sleuthing," Malee remarked.

"I'm sure the time wasn't wasted," Louise said. "We may have picked up a clue. Anyway, we must be very careful."

Mr. Wongsuwan agreed. "We will say nothing until the proper time." He smiled at the Danas and added, "There is an old Siamese proverb which states: 'If you do not hear the story clearly, do not carry it off with you under your arm.' "

Nevertheless, Mr. Wongsuwan admitted that the

whole incident looked very suspicious. He promised to keep a close watch on his son-in-law and Thongchai. Malee's father even remarked that he did not want his daughter Pratoom to continue living with a man who proved not to be completely trustworthy.

Boonmi made no other stops, except at a boat where Thongchai bought some fruit. The followers watched eagerly to see what he would pay for them. But this time he handed over only coins.

When he reached the river, Boonmi turned toward home. This was not, the Danas knew, in the direction of the klong where the bamboo birds were made. Sure that Boonmi and Thongchai had accomplished their morning's mission, Louise suggested that the group continue sleuthing.

"If you have time, Mr. Wongsuwan," she said, "would you please go with us to the place where the little boy said bamboo birds like Malee's are being made? You may have more luck than we did getting inside the house."

Malee's father said he doubted it, but he would be very glad to try. He turned the motorboat, and followed the Danas' directions. To their embarrassment, they took him up the wrong klong, but he good-naturedly turned the boat and piloted the craft to another canal.

This one proved to be the right stream. Nobody was outside the suspected house, so Malee's father stepped from the boat and went to the front door.

Instantly a man appeared and a long conversation in Thai took place. Finally Mr. Wongsuwan came back to the boat and started off.

"I am afraid I am not a very good detective," he remarked wryly. "The man was annoyed and kept repeating that he was too busy to waste time with strangers."

"Never mind," said Jean. "You did the best you could, Mr. Wongsuwan."

"If we are too persistent," Malee's father said, "the people may move their whole project away, and it might be difficult then to find out where the work is going on."

The girls knew this was true, and Jean suggested, "Maybe we'd better tell the police."

"Please, not yet," Mr. Wongsuwan requested. He was inclined to agree with the Danas' suspicions of the Chamnans' place, but he felt they should wait until they had more proof before reporting the matter to the authorities.

"We'll respect your wishes, Mr. Wongsuwan," Jean conceded, knowing he feared unfavorable publicity.

The group returned to the Oriental Hotel. As Louise and Jean were about to step from the boat, Malee said, "My father has arranged a surprise for you and your aunt. Tomorrow you will fly into Cambodia to see the ancient ruins of Angkor Thom and Angkor Wat."

"How exciting!" the sisters cried out together.

Malee's father smiled. "I hope you do not mind leaving very early in the morning. The hotel clerk will call you at four A.M."

"Four!" Jean exclaimed, then added, "But I wouldn't miss it for anything. Thank you very, very much, Mr. Wongsuwan."

Louise added her thanks, not only for the forthcoming trip, but for the one that morning. Then the sisters hurried up to the hotel.

As they entered the lobby the girls saw Aunt Harriet seated near the garden. After kissing them good morning, she said, "I want to hear all about your adventure."

Just then, a boy carrying a package came toward the Danas. Louise and Jean recognized him as the youngster who had had the bamboo Garuda bird in his boat.

"I make you present," he said in halting English as he handed Louise the package. "Thank you. Good-by."

Without another word he ran across the lobby and disappeared out the door.

CHAPTER XVII

# Fugitive Suspect

"WASN'T that cute of him?" Jean said, gazing after the boy's disappearing figure. "What do you suppose is in the package?"

Aunt Harriet was dubiously eying the crudely wrapped box. "I'm not sure you should open it. We have no idea what's inside. It could be something dangerous."

"Oh, I don't think that darling boy would do such a thing," Louise protested.

"He may not even know what's in the box," Aunt Harriet persisted. "Some older person might have asked him to deliver it and to say exactly what he did."

Louise held the package to her ear, then remarked with a smile that there was no ticking. "So there's no time bomb inside!" She giggled.

"Let's compromise," Jean suggested. "We'll carry the box outside and open it carefully without touching the contents. Then, if anything is going to pop up or fly out or spray us with anything harmful, we'll have a chance to get back some distance from it."

By this time Aunt Harriet had relented a bit, and thought this procedure would be safe. They walked outside. Cautiously Louise slipped the loose cord off the wrapping with a long comb from her purse, then unfolded the paper with the comb. She pushed up the lid of the box.

The three Danas were prepared to jump back. Instead they burst into laughter. Inside the box lay a crudely fashioned bamboo Garuda bird! Evidently the boy had made it himself. The bird was about five inches long, and not gilded or painted.

"I think it was sweet of that boy to do this," Louise said. "And he didn't wait to be thanked!"

"We'll never be able to find him in this big city!" Jean lamented. "He figured we wanted a bird, so he put one together himself."

She lifted the bird from the box and looked to see if it had an opening. It did not. Furthermore, the bamboo object was so light she was sure there was nothing inside.

Louise took the bird from her sister and examined it carefully. Convinced it was a harmless toy, she slipped it into her handbag.

Meanwhile, Jean had picked up the box and wrappings, and carried them to the doorman for disposal. As the Danas re-entered the hotel, Aunt

Harriet said, "How about some breakfast? You girls must be starved."

"We've had our fruit," said Jean with a chuckle. "No less than four bananas each!"

As they ate breakfast, the sisters told Aunt Harriet about the morning's adventure and that Thongchai was now a suspect.

Aunt Harriet frowned. "That is a bad situation—a master and his servant apparently both in some scheme. But maybe you're wrong. Boonmi and Thongchai may be entirely innocent."

"Perhaps," Jean spoke up, "but personally I don't think Malee and her sister would be suspicious without some good reason."

"Yes," Louise agreed, "and I feel that we know practically nothing of the real story."

The girls told their aunt of the proposed trip into Cambodia the next day by air. She looked pleased. "A visit to the old ruins in the jungle sounds fascinating. And there's another thing I like. For one day at least you'll be away from this Bangkok mystery and entirely safe. Nothing too dangerous has happened to you so far, but your sleuthing worries me just the same."

Jean's eyes twinkled as she changed the subject. "Aunt Harriet, what's the earliest you've ever arisen in the morning?"

Miss Dana smiled. "The night before," she answered, "meaning that I have stayed up the whole night—never went to bed at all."

"When was this?" Jean asked. "At college?"

Aunt Harriet laughed. "That was one of the times. The other was when your Uncle Ned was very ill and I was playing night nurse. Why?"

"Because tomorrow you'll have to get up at four A.M.," Jean told her.

Aunt Harriet made a wry face but said she would be ready. Then she suggested that the three of them do a little sightseeing.

"Where would you like to go?" Louise asked.

"Across the river to the Temple of Dawn. I believe it's called the Wat Arun," Aunt Harriet answered.

"That's a grand idea," said Louise. "We'll rent a boat and go over there."

An hour later they set off and found a handsome guide with a sturdy motorboat. He said his name was Khan, and he agreed to take them sightseeing on the river, then to the Wat Arun.

The Danas climbed aboard and Khan headed out into the river. In a little while he drew up alongside two beautiful golden barges.

"These are the royal barges," Khan explained. "The king and queen ride in them on ceremonial occasions."

Aunt Harriet and the girls saw that each vessel had a roofed section in the middle for its royal occupant. The ends of the craft, which would accommodate some thirty-six rowers, curved high into the air. The prow of the king's boat was shaped like a warrior, while the queen's was a beautiful swan.

"Because ladies are supposed to be graceful as swans," the guide explained with a smile.

Presently they reached the dock of the Wat Arun where several motorboats were tied up. The Danas gazed in awe at the massive structure. The temple was built layer upon layer and towered some two hundred feet. Each tier had a platform which appeared to be held up by carved figures of mythological creatures. The rest of the edifice was decorated with designs made from pieces of broken porcelain which glittered in the sunlight.

"You like it?" Khan asked, smiling. When they exclaimed over its beauty, he went on, "We are very proud of this temple. As you can see, it has tremendous weight, yet is built on piles driven into the mud. The engineering was so perfect that the building has not moved one-half inch in fifty years!"

"That is amazing!" Aunt Harriet murmured in admiration.

"Do you wish to climb up the steps?" the guide asked.

"Oh, yes," Louise said immediately.

She and Jean scampered up. Aunt Harriet and Khan followed more slowly. The girls paused on the first landing, before going on to the next one. Aunt Harriet got this far, then said she felt she had done enough climbing for the day. She would look around a bit, then go down to the ground level.

Her nieces continued to climb, admiring not only the Wat Arun but the wonderful scene of the temples and river life spread out below. As they approached another tier, Louise and Jean saw a Buddhist priest talking to a stocky man. Both men had their backs toward the girls, but hearing the sound of footsteps, the one wearing a business suit turned around.

Jean and Louise gasped. The stocky man was the one they thought to be Swad Holden!

The girls waited until the priest had finished his conversation and walked off, then they hurried up to the suspect. "You are Mr. Swad Holden, are you not?" Jean asked.

The man did not reply. His eyes narrowed as he looked at the girls malevolently. Suddenly he pushed past them and started down the steps at top speed.

"He must be Holden!" Louise whispered. "Let's go after him!"

The fugitive had a slight head start, but the girls were right back of him. The descent was dangerous at a fast pace, and though Jean and Louise tried running down the steps diagonally to avoid falling, they found that their quarry continued his mad dash, heedless of a possible headlong tumble.

"He'll get away!" Jean panted.

Louise nodded. She would get Aunt Harriet and Khan to help them catch Holden.

"Khan! Stop this man!" Louise cried out, and Jean added, "Aunt Harriet! Don't let him get away! He's the one we've been trying to find!"

The two watchers below, alerted, stood ready to frustrate the fugitive's attempt to escape. But Swad Holden was cunning. Reaching one of the landings, he turned abruptly and disappeared.

The girls ran after him. Reaching the corner, they saw Holden racing down a different flight of steps. In a moment he turned again, once more disappearing from sight. Although Louise and Jean looked on all sides of the Wat Arun, they were unable to spot him.

"He escaped!" Jean said in disgust, as she and Louise went down to the bottom of the steps.

When Aunt Harriet and Khan appeared, they too reported no luck in locating the suspect. Just then, Louise noticed an American sightseer strolling in their direction. At once she asked him if he had seen a stocky man running away from the temple.

"Yes, I did. He was headed for the dock."

"Thank you."

The group set off on a run for the waterfront. When they reached it, Khan rapidly glanced around. "One of the motorboats that was here before is missing," he declared. "There it is, part way across the river!" He pointed.

The suspect continued his mad dash.

"Let's follow it!" Jean urged.

The Danas and their guide quickly jumped into their boat. The motor roared and Khan sped across the river.

The boat they were pursuing stopped at the Oriental Hotel. As its pilot leaped out, Jean cried, "That *is* Holden! Let's hurry!"

The stocky man raced toward the street, and by the time Khan reached the dock, Holden was nowhere in sight.

"No use to look for him now," the young guide remarked. "Too many places to hide."

The girls admitted their defeat. Khan eyed them quizzically and asked why they wanted to catch the man.

The Danas looked at one another. It seemed best not to tell the whole story, but Louise said with a smile, "We go to a girls' private school in America. We think the man we're chasing caused a fire that almost destroyed part of the school."

"That is too bad," Khan remarked, bobbing his head sympathetically.

At that moment a Thai gentleman rushed up and began speaking rapidly in his native tongue to Khan. Presently the Danas' guide translated.

"Someone stole this man's motorboat from here. It is the one we were chasing."

"I speak English," the stranger said. "What did this thief look like?"

After the girls had given a full description and said they thought his name was Swad Holden, the stranger held up his hands in despair and cried out:

"I know about that man. He is a wicked person! He stole jewels from my shop!"

CHAPTER XVIII

# Wild Elephant Ride

IRATE, the Bangkok jeweler continued, "I have report that man to the police once. I do it again. You say his name may be Swad Holden?"

"We think it is," Louise said. "When did the theft in your shop occur?"

"Yesterday. This man came in and looked at my finest rubies. He did not buy, but after he left I learn some of the gems were missing."

"That's too bad," Jean put in. "I certainly hope Mr. Holden will be caught soon. And I'm glad you got your boat back."

"I will lock it up this time," the jeweler declared. He bowed to the Danas. "I thank you for helping me know about the thief."

He climbed into his craft, waved good-by, and with a smile started off down the river.

The Danas' guide said, "It would give me great pleasure to help you ladies catch the thief."

"Thank you. We should like that," said Louise. She grinned. "Have *you* any idea where Mr. Holden might have gone?"

Their guide smiled and admitted that he had not, but if Holden had stolen jewelry with him, he might be headed for one of the gem-setting factories or shops to sell them. "Would you like to go to them? I know every place."

The girls were thinking fast. No doubt the police were already covering such spots. But another idea came into Louise's mind, which she felt should be reported.

"*Holden might be a smuggler!*" she whispered to Jean.

Jean agreed. "And using the bamboo birds to secrete gems." She explained they probably were embedded between layers of the wood. The attractive and unusual birds could even be sent out under the guise of toys to confederates of Holden's in the United States or other countries.

"I think we should report seeing Holden to the police," Louise said aloud, without explaining further to Khan.

"I will show you the way there," the guide replied affably. "Shall we take a taxi?"

The Danas smiled and nodded. They had not yet ridden in one of these rickshas pulled by a man on a three-wheeled bicycle. Their guide found two of the quaint pedicabs. He rode with Aunt Harriet, while the sisters followed in a second taxi.

"This is a smooth method of travel," Aunt Harriet remarked.

In the other pedicab Louise and Jean whispered about their latest hunch that Swad Holden was a smuggler.

"How much do you think we should tell the police of our suspicions?" Jean asked.

"Nothing that would involve the Wongsuwan family or Boonmi or Thongchai," Louise replied. "But I think it would be all right to tell the police about the house where the bamboo birds are being made."

The taxis took the Danas and their guide up a fine broad avenue lined with Bangkok's modern and attractive buildings. Presently they came to police headquarters.

As diplomatically as possible, Jean distracted Khan's attention while Louise asked Aunt Harriet if she would mind waiting outside with the young man.

"I understand. You don't want him to hear your story." Aunt Harriet smiled, then asked Khan if he would show her the grounds.

He bowed, grinned, and said, "I will be happy to do this."

Louise and Jean went inside and soon were talking to one of the law-enforcement officers. Nai Pong, who spoke excellent English, was amazed at their story and said he would have detectives watch the Chamnans' place.

"It may be that Swad Holden will come there," he said. "We have been unable to locate him and cannot understand it. Many policemen are looking for this man."

"We believe," Louise told him, "that Mr. Holden has recently disguised himself in New York as a Far Eastern prince. Perhaps at times he has masqueraded in Bangkok also. This may be the reason he cannot be found." She smiled. "We do know that he smokes Weathervane cigarettes and throws them around carelessly."

"I thank you for what you Americans call a good tip," Officer Nai Pong said. "We will keep it in mind."

When the girls returned to the street, Aunt Harriet and Khan had finished their tour of the grounds. "We will stop at a Chinese market," the guide said, then directed the taximen to one.

After a short ride, the pedicabs pulled up to an open-front market. Alighting, the Danas entered and gazed about in fascination.

"Why, it's like a general store at home!" Jean exclaimed. "But how different the articles are!"

Among the more exotic items for sale were dried and smoked bats, spices of various kinds, lacquered duckskins, and incense batons.

"Fun to look at," Louise remarked, "but I don't think I want a smoked bat for lunch!"

"Speaking of lunch," Aunt Harriet said, "it's about time for ours."

The Danas thanked Khan for the morning's tour, then returned to the Oriental Hotel. At luncheon Aunt Harriet was told of the conversation in the police station. She praised her nieces for not having mentioned the Wongsuwans in connection with the mystery.

"If Boonmi is involved," she said, "it would be far better that he be exposed by other people than ourselves, since we are in a way guests of Malee's parents."

Because the day was very hot, the Danas decided to spend the afternoon in their rooms writing letters. Aunt Harriet wrote to Uncle Ned, Louise to her special friend Ken Scott, and Jean to Chris Barton whom she often dated.

The Danas went to bed at eight o'clock that evening in order to feel alert at four the next morning. Nevertheless, they found it difficult to get up when the time came. At four-fifteen there was a knock on the girls' door, and the room boy brought breakfast.

After he had gone, Jean said with a giggle, "We're not the only ones to lose sleep. It seems as if that poor boy is on duty at all hours!"

When the Danas reached the airport, they found that the special plane going to Siem Reap in Cambodia was filled with sightseeing passengers. An hour and a half later the pilot spoke over the loudspeaker in several languages. In English he said that the great ruins of Angkor Thom and Angkor Wat could be seen below.

The Danas gazed out the window. From a dense woods rose a series of buildings with innumerable stately towers.

"I understand," said Aunt Harriet, "that these buildings were started around A.D. 900 and were added to way up through the twelfth century."

"They're magnificent!" Jean exclaimed. "Isn't it wicked that they were partly destroyed?"

"That always is such a dreadful part of war," Aunt Harriet replied. "Why can't conquerors leave intact the fine things which men have created?"

After the plane had taxied to a stop, the sightseers were led to buses. There was a pleasant ride along a muddy river. But the inhabitants apparently did not mind its color! Children were playing, and grownups swimming about.

Jean laughed. "I'm so hot, I'd almost rather be going for a swim than looking at jungle ruins. It's about twice as hot here as in Bangkok."

After a while the buses stopped in a shady area where women and small boys were selling silver souvenir replicas of carvings, which, they said, appeared on the buildings. Men offered large straw hats and the Danas purchased three for protection from the sun.

A guide who was waiting to direct the group spoke. "The ancient city of Angkor covered sixty square miles. Today you will see some of its beauty.

This morning I will show you part of the ruins of Angkor Thom which contained many remarkable buildings. All of them are fine examples of the old Khmer architecture of this area. You will find it necessary to do a good bit of climbing up and down the old steps. Watch carefully."

"Do we have to walk there?" Aunt Harriet asked, looking through a maze of gnarled trees to the ancient, crumbling buildings in front of them.

As the guide nodded, the Danas suddenly heard a shout. Turning, they saw an elephant plodding toward them, a native mahout guiding the animal from his perch on its neck. The tourists stared as he looked them over.

Finally, fastening his eyes on Louise and Jean, who were the only girls in the group, he called, "Your name Dana?"

"Yes, it is," Louise answered in surprise.

The mahout leaned forward. "I have job to give you ride to main sight in Angkor Thom. It is Temple of Bayon. I help you climb up."

The three Danas gazed at the man in utter astonishment, then Aunt Harriet asked, "Who told you to give us a ride?"

The mahout smiled. "Telephone call from man in Bangkok name of Wongsuwan. He make arrangements. Very gentle elephant, he say."

"Oh, a ride on an elephant would be fun!" Jean cried. "Let's try it!"

Aunt Harriet shook her head. "If you girls want

to, all right, but I think I'll walk. I'll meet you at the Bayon Temple."

The mahout had jumped down. With his stick he tapped the elephant's front legs. The huge beast dropped to its knees, and with the man's help, the girls scrambled up the elephant's trunk to the howdah on its back.

"Aunt Harriet, you don't mind if Jean and I leave you?" Louise called down.

"No. Go ahead." Aunt Harriet laughed. "But don't fall off!"

The other sightseers waved and called good-by as the sisters started away, with the mahout once more in position on the beast's neck.

The driver did not take the same route that the foot guide had picked for the sightseers. Instead, he went deeper into the jungle. About three hundred yards from the road the mahout suddenly mumbled something in his own language, stopped the elephant, and slid to the ground.

"What's the matter?" Louise questioned.

The mahout did not reply. He walked to the rear of his elephant. As the girls were about to turn around to see what he was doing, the beast suddenly raised its trunk into the air, trumpeted angrily, and started to run.

Louise and Jean grabbed the sides of the howdah and tried their best to hang on. But the elephant, infuriated by something, began to gallop. Louise's purse flew from her hand, opened in mid-air, and all the contents fell out, including the small bamboo bird which was still in it.

"Wh-what shall we do?" Jean shouted worriedly.

Louise was grim. As the huge beast crashed at full speed through the jungle, she knew that they were in imminent danger of being thrown off and possibly trampled as well!

CHAPTER XIX

# False Messages

"WE—we'd—better swing onto some tr-tr-tree branches!" Louise managed to say. She realized that if she and Jean did not save themselves from the rampaging elephant, it might be too late.

"G-good i-idea," her sister gasped.

Most of the branches on the giant fromage trees were out of reach, but finally the girls saw a lower one ahead. Just before coming to it, they raised their arms, stood up, and sprang to grasp the branch. It was a tense moment. The girls wondered if the elephant, in his disturbed state, might turn back and strike them with his trunk. But he plunged on, trumpeting loudly.

Louise and Jean pulled themselves up onto the stout branch and looked at each other in relief. With a forced grin Jean said, "That was a lucky break!"

"Yes, but we're not out of trouble yet," Louise

reminded her. "We still have to get down and that isn't going to be easy."

"We'll just have to shin down," said Jean.

She inched along the branch to the trunk and flung her arms about it. Jean could not quite stretch them all the way around the giant tree.

"I'm going to try going down, anyway," she declared.

Louise watched fearfully as her sister made her way down the trunk, sliding, digging in with her heels, but finally reaching the bottom. Her arms and legs were bruised and bleeding. "But at least I'm safe," Jean thought gratefully.

Her sister also descended unharmed. On the ground at last, she complained, "That mahout wasn't worried about us. He hasn't come to find out what happened."

"Louise," said Jean suddenly, "do you think it's possible that fellow made the elephant run away on purpose?"

Her sister looked startled. "But why?"

Jean shrugged. "Maybe he just doesn't like tourists. Well, let's follow the elephant's trail back and pick up your purse and the stuff that spilled out of it."

"I hope there aren't any poisonous snakes around," said Louise. "We'd better steer clear of rocks and logs."

The girls made their way back cautiously, following the elephant's footprints. There was no sign of the mahout. They wondered where he had gone.

Finally Louise found her purse, and together the girls picked up what they could find of the scattered contents. Louise discovered her wallet some little distance from the other articles. The money had been taken from it.

"I guess robbery was the mahout's motive," she told Jean. "He just wanted to make the whole thing look like an accident."

"Say, the little bamboo bird isn't around," Jean remarked. "Do you suppose the mahout took that too?"

"I suppose so," Louise answered. "But I don't see the point. It wasn't valuable."

Jean said she was thoroughly suspicious now that there was more to the episode than the theft of the money. "This may be a wild guess, but maybe there's a tie-in between the mahout and the Bangkok makers of the Garuda birds. This Cambodian knows about them, but probably hasn't seen the valuable birds. He took ours, thinking it would prove to the higher-ups that we have found out too much."

"But, Jean," said Louise, puzzled, "surely Mr. Wongsuwan wouldn't have engaged the mahout to cause the accident!"

"No," Jean agreed, "but someone who overheard him arranging the elephant ride may have added the other order to it."

"I suppose we can't find out anything more until we return to Bangkok," Louise said. "Well, let's join Aunt Harriet."

The girls started their trek back to the entrance of the ancient city. On the way they found a spring bubbling out of the ground. Louise and Jean stopped to wash their faces, hands, and legs, and comb their hair.

"I guess there isn't much we can do about our clothes." Louise gave a sigh.

It was nearly half an hour later before the girls found Aunt Harriet at the Temple of Bayon in the center of the ruined ancient city of Angkor.

"What in the world happened to you?" she gasped, looking in dismay at her nieces' disheveled appearance and cuts and bruises.

Quickly they whispered to her what had happened, but advised that they keep the details from the other sightseers.

"We can just say we had an unusual elephant ride." Jean grinned.

"And then let's talk about this fabulous building," Louise suggested.

The Bayon Temple had several towers. On each side of these were enormous carved human faces, each one different, and probably representing kings, warriors, or priests of long ago.

"They're remarkably well preserved," Aunt Harriet noted.

"Yes," Louise agreed. "It's too bad that this

whole city can't be rebuilt and lived in again. It must have been very beautiful."

"No doubt," said Jean. "But it would cost a fortune to restore it."

When the morning's sightseeing was over, the visitors were taken to the Grand Hotel D'Angkor, where they were to have lunch. Louise thought the elephant incident should be reported to the police without further delay, so the girls called the Siem Reap station. The officer in charge listened in amazement and apologized profusely for his countryman's unseemly actions.

"I will investigate the matter at once," he stated. "It should not be too difficult to find this dishonorable mahout."

"Thank you," said Louise, then she and Jean joined the others at luncheon.

After a short rest, the bus drivers announced they were ready to leave for Angkor Wat. On the way, they explained that the huge temple was built by King Suryavarman in the middle of the twelfth century. It had originally been surrounded by a high wall, and protected by lotus-filled moats. The temple had been dedicated to the Hindu god Vishnu of the Brahman sect. The religion had been brought to Cambodia from India.

When the buses reached the main entrance, the sightseers started the quarter-mile walk along a flagstone-paved causeway to the temple.

Aunt Harriet looked ahead at the treeless walk,

and remarked that it was certainly going to be a very hot trek. "The temperature must be near a hundred," she surmised. "And the sun is blazing."

The girls suggested that she wait in the shade of the jungle trees, but Aunt Harriet added quickly, "Oh, I wouldn't miss this for anything!"

The causeway, which led over a moat, had stone sides with carved, snakelike balustrades.

"The snakes are called *nagas*," the guide explained.

When the Danas reached the temple, they were astounded by the length and height of the rectangular building. It was three stories high, and everywhere one looked there were carved groups of figures depicted on the stonework. Each group told a story: some were of war, some of duels; and others were tragically humorous, as was one of an unfortunate victim falling out of a boat into the mouth of a crocodile!

The sightseers picked their way among the ruins, climbing, taking pictures, and pausing to gaze through avenues of rooms once inhabited by priests. With the passage of centuries, the ruined buildings had fallen prey to jungle animals and reptiles and to the mammoth banyan trees which pushed their branches between the huge blocks of stone.

"The power of nature always amazes me," Aunt Harriet remarked. "After all, it is stronger than anything man can build!"

They left Angkor Wat, and the bus took them to other uncovered ruins in the jungle. Louise and Jean were fascinated by the Terrace of the Elephants. Their guide said this probably had been the foundation of a great entertainment hall, annexed to the king's palace, but the building was gone. Almost as far as the girls could see, along the high foundation wall were carvings of life-size elephants. Most of the beasts faced forward, their trunks extended. Some were eating lotuses, while others appeared to be hunting with their masters.

"What intricate work!" Aunt Harriet exclaimed. "There must have been many artists among the million inhabitants here."

Soon it was time for the sightseers to leave. Weary and hot, they were glad to board the air-conditioned plane, relax in the comfortable seats, and return to Bangkok. As soon as the Danas reached their hotel rooms, Louise telephoned Mr. Wongsuwan. She thanked him for arranging the marvelous excursion, then asked:

"Did you order an elephant ride for Jean and me while we were at Siem Reap?"

"No, Louise, I did not. Why do you ask?"

Louise told the whole story, and Mr. Wongsuwan was greatly disturbed. "Someone deliberately used my name!" he said. "The runaway ride was planned to injure you girls. I shall communicate with the local police at once!"

Louise said good-by, then reported this latest development in the mystery to her sister and aunt. They agreed that the person responsible for the elephant ride had used Mr. Wongsuwan's name as a cover-up.

"I'll bet it was Boonmi!" Jean stormed, jumping up and pacing the floor with her hands behind her back.

"Or Thongchai," Louise suggested.

Aunt Harriet had still another idea. "It might have been Swad Holden. He is a linguist and no doubt speaks French, which is used in Cambodia as well as the native language."

Just then the telephone rang. Jean hurried to answer.

"Is this Miss Dana?" a strange male voice asked.

"Yes," Jean replied. Then, as she listened, her eyes widened. "Thank you," she said. "We'll come immediately."

As she put down the telephone she turned to Louise and Aunt Harriet. "That was the police department," she explained. "They have news for us which they can't tell over the phone. They want us to come to headquarters at once!"

"Let's go!" Louise cried. The three grabbed their purses and hurried from the room.

The Danas found a taxi standing at the hotel entrance. They climbed in and Jean directed the driver to police headquarters.

Before he could start the motor, a man and woman dashed from the hotel and crowded into the front seat beside the driver, speaking excitedly in Thai. The taximan drove off.

The girls weren't sure, but it seemed to them that he was going in the wrong direction. Louise queried the driver.

"I am sorry, miss, but I must take this gentleman and his wife home at once. We will go there first."

Fifteen minutes later he pulled into the long driveway of a new, modern home, quite secluded from the street. He stopped at the entrance and the couple alighted.

Suddenly the man passenger yanked open the rear door and said harshly to the Danas, "Get out and march inside the house!"

"Why, what do you mean?" Louise demanded in astonishment.

"Just do as I say!"

"How absurd!" Aunt Harriet exclaimed. "Driver, aren't you going to do something about this?"

The taximan turned around and leered at Aunt Harriet and her nieces. "You'd better do what you're told or you'll get hurt."

"But the telephone call from the police?" Jean asked. "Was that a fake?"

"That was me," he said with a self-satisfied grin.

The Danas were frightened, but not ready to give up so easily. Jean began to yell for help at the top of her voice.

Instantly the man holding the door clapped a

hand over her mouth and dragged her from the cab, then the driver pulled Louise out, and the woman guarded Aunt Harriet.

Two other men came out of the house, and the Danas knew their capture was inevitable. They were prisoners of an unknown enemy!

CHAPTER XX

# The Secret Exit

As THE taxi drove off, the three Danas were shoved through the front door by the woman and her three male companions.

"This is an outrage!" Aunt Harriet cried. "Take your hands off me! What is this all about?"

"You will find out soon enough," one of the men said. "Get up those stairs!"

Unable to do otherwise, the sisters and their aunt walked up the broad steps of the attractive, well-furnished house. From a window on the stairway, Louise could see the outline of the great Wat Arun across the river.

"How long are you going to keep us prisoners?" Jean demanded. "And why?"

The man who had been in the taxi laughed. "In Thailand one is never impatient. If you are co-operative, you will be treated well. My friends and I have work to do. We do not know how long it will take. You will be here until it is accomplished. That may be one month, two—perhaps six."

"Six months!" the three Danas were horrified.

This time there was no response from their captors. Aunt Harriet and the girls were ushered into a very pleasant second-floor bedroom with private bath. There were three single beds. Instantly Jean rushed to the window, hoping to find some means of escape. But to her dismay she found that it did not open. The room was air-conditioned.

"I hope you ladies will be comfortable," another of the men, evidently a servant, said. "I will bring you some food in a little while."

The men and their female companion went into the hall. The door to the Danas' room was closed and locked.

"What are we going to do?" Aunt Harriet exclaimed woefully.

"I'll think of something," Louise promised her, but in her heart the girl felt that the situation was pretty hopeless.

Nevertheless, she and Jean began a thorough search of the room and its adjoining bath. The girls had not gone far when they heard the clank of a key in the lock. A moment later the door opened. The man they had suspected of being Swad Holden walked in.

He smiled smugly at the group. "We meet again," he said suavely, "but this time you are not chasing me."

The Danas were silent, waiting coldly for him to continue. Sensing their animosity, his voice began to ring with hatred. "You girls have been too clever," he said. "It is time you were punished. You have ruined a great money-making scheme of mine."

As he paused, Louise put in accusingly, "You mean smuggling gems out of the country in bamboo birds?"

"Yes. But Swad Holden is not a man to be trifled with. Another plan will present itself soon, but you shall remain here until it is put into successful operation."

Between questions from the sisters and admissions on Holden's part, Louise, Jean, and Aunt Harriet were able to confirm their suspicions about the man. He was an international jewel thief.

While in Bangkok, Holden had learned that Malee's father had had the exquisite gilded bamboo Garuda bird, containing a jeweled Buddha, made for his daughter to take to school in the United States. He had determined to obtain it.

"I wanted to use the bird as a model," he said. "First I made detailed drawings of the bird, then I disguised myself as a Far Eastern prince and sold the Garuda to a Fifth Avenue jeweler."

"What did you do with the Buddha?" Jean asked.

"I kept it. I put the cheap golden chedi inside the bamboo Garuda to mislead you just in case you found the bird."

Holden admitted that Thongchai was a henchman of his. It was through the servant, who had overheard Pratoom talking to Boonmi, that he had learned by cable that Malee and the Danas were coming to Bangkok.

Thongchai had cleverly induced his employer to talk freely about every bit of sightseeing the Danas were to do. It was he who had engaged the two vegetable-boatmen to push the Dana girls under water in order to scare them away from further detective work.

"Were you the one who arranged our special elephant ride in Cambodia?" Louise inquired angrily.

"Yes. If that plan had worked, you might never have come back."

Aunt Harriet's eyes blazed. "You are a very wicked man," she said.

Holden chuckled. "Many people have called me that, but it does not worry me."

He admitted that when Thongchai had not been able to glean enough information about the Danas' sightseeing excursions, he himself, disguised as a woman, had shadowed the girls. At other times, he had a stooge of his, the taxi driver, trail the girls for him.

"That was how I knew you were going to the Wat Arun," he explained. "I had it all set up to push you down those long steps. But you got there ahead of my taxi friend who was going to help me and spoiled my plan. But you won't spoil any more!"

Louise changed the subject. "When you stole the Garuda at Starhurst did you throw away a burning cigarette in the main part of the building?"

Holden admitted that he had entered the school through a window in the main section and was smoking at the time. "My cigarette may have set the building on fire, but I did not do it on purpose."

"Did you try to make trouble for Malee and the girls in Honolulu?" Aunt Harriet spoke up.

"Oh, yes," Holden replied with a smirk. "I sent a fake cable so you would stay with the Punyarachoons rather than at a hotel. And one of my pals and I created the disturbance that night—I screamed to attract attention so he could get into the house. He was going to unlock the door later, so we could kidnap Miss Wongsuwan to keep you girls from coming to Bangkok."

"I'm glad that sinister plot failed," Aunt Harriet said, her eyes blazing.

All this time the Danas were wondering if Holden would mention Boonmi as one of his accomplices. They did not want to ask the direct question. Finally Louise said:

"The day we were in the palace grounds, you called to Mr. Boonruang Kinaree. Were you sending a message to his servant?"

"That is exactly right," Holden answered. "But the note I gave him for Thongchai was in code.

Boonruang knows nothing of our smuggling operation."

A great feeling of relief came over the Danas that Pratoom's husband was innocent of any wrongdoing.

Suddenly Holden laughed. "As a matter of fact," he said, "part of my scheme was to make you suspect Boonmi."

"How did you manage that?" Jean asked.

"I had Thongchai drop a hint to Boonmi even before you girls arrived that you were schemers. He said that you were probably trying to get Malee to talk her father into giving you a large sum of money for solving the mystery of the stolen bamboo bird, but you were doing nothing to find it. Later Thongchai added that you would probably blackmail the family, by spreading some wild story about them being involved in a smuggling racket."

Aunt Harriet gasped. "You really are a vicious person!" she said disdainfully.

Holden smirked in satisfaction. "That is a harsh word, Miss Dana. Let us just say that I am clever—cleverer than most people and certainly more so than the ones who have tried to trip me up." He looked triumphantly at Louise and Jean.

"Did you also make Boonmi's wife suspicious about him in regard to money matters?" Louise asked.

"Yes, I did that too. Thongchai left fake I O U's where she would find them. Once he let her find a receipt for the sale of a necklace of hers which I had stolen. It had the initials P. K. on it."

"You despicable person!" Jean burst out.

There was a knock on the door. "Someone to see you, Mr. Holden," a voice called.

As Holden left, another man brought in three food trays piled one above the other. He set them on a small table in the room, then left without a word. The door was locked again.

"I hope there isn't poison in this food." Jean gazed distrustfully at the tempting array of dishes. "I'll try a tiny bit."

She picked up a small piece of chicken and put it into her mouth. A second later Jean took it out, gasping "Ugh! This must have been boiled in hot pepper!"

She, Aunt Harriet, and Louise tried the other foods one by one, with the same result. Everything was so highly spiced, the Danas could eat none of it.

"At this rate we'll starve to death!" Jean wailed.

Louise drew her aunt and sister close to her. "This is all the more reason why we'll *have* to escape somehow," she said, and gazed around the room. Suddenly her eyes lighted up. "This is a new house," Louise observed. "Maybe it was built by Holden and his friends. One thing they'd think of is escape for themselves in case they needed to leave in a hurry. Let's look for sliding panels and a trap door."

All three Danas set to work excitedly. Louise had her eye on a tall built-in wardrobe. She opened the door and examined the walls. To her complete delight she found that the series of panels at the rear moved.

*There was an opening beyond into another wardrobe!*

A telephone rang in the adjoining room. Her heart leaped in exultation. If they could not escape from the house, at least they might be able to phone the police for help!

Someone opened the hall door in the adjoining room and came to answer the phone. There was a lengthy conversation in Thai, then the man hung up, left, and once more closed the door to the hall.

"Now's my chance!" Louise thought.

By this time Jean and Aunt Harriet had come to see what she had discovered. There was a quick whispered conversation and plans were made: Louise and Jean would go into the far room, with Jean standing guard at the door; Aunt Harriet would remain in their own room, while Louise called the police. Swiftly the sisters made their way forward and Jean took her position.

Louise picked up the phone and listened. The wire was not in use. In a low but distinct voice she said to the operator, "Police headquarters!"

Within seconds, the call was put through. Louise asked if Officer Nai Pong was there. A few more seconds passed before the man answered.

"This is Louise Dana," the girl said quickly. "My aunt and sister and I are prisoners. We're on the second floor of a new house about a quarter of a mile from the river. From the rear of the house we can see the Wat Arun."

The girls heard footsteps in the hall. Louise dared not wait for a response and hung up instantly. The sisters dashed back through the wardrobe, quickly sliding the panels into place. Just as they reached their own room, still breathless, the hall door was opened.

It was Thongchai. The Danas looked at him in disgust.

"I understand you young ladies know the whole story about me," Thongchai said. "But it will do you no good. Months from now, when you are free, I shall be far, far away from here. I will no longer be a servant, but a very wealthy man."

The Danas did not antagonize the man. Instead, Aunt Harriet said, "We cannot eat this food. It is too spicy. Will you please see that we get something that is more palatable."

"Anything to make your visit enjoyable," Thongchai sneered. "What would you like?"

Louise and Jean realized their aunt was trying to keep him in the house until the police arrived. The girls began a lengthy conversation, mentioning all kinds of attractive American foods. Fortunately, the man seemed to be interested and in no hurry to leave.

Fifteen minutes had elapsed when the Danas and Thongchai heard a commotion and loud voices from the first floor of the house. Thongchai called to the guard in the hall to let him out. There was no answer.

"What's going on here?" he demanded.

The Danas remained silent. Their hearts were pounding in suspense. Had help arrived? Thongchai beat frantically on the door. Still no response. The furor below grew louder. Thongchai pounded and kicked the door like a raving maniac. Apparently he knew nothing of the secret opening in the wardrobe.

A few minutes later they heard footsteps in the hall, and a key turning in the lock. The door burst open. Thongchai was about to say something when his face turned ashen. He was confronted by Officer Nai Pong and several other men in uniform.

"The police!" he cried out, backing away.

"Yes. We have arrested your friends," the officer told him sternly. "You come along with me."

Thongchai had no alternative. He was led downstairs by two policemen. Officer Nai Pong turned to the Danas.

"How can the Bangkok authorities ever thank you for your fine work? You have helped us capture a long-wanted smuggling group, and at great risk to yourselves."

The Danas were almost too overcome with relief

to speak, but Louise said, "We have *you* to thank for rescuing us."

Nai Pong said that he would get in touch with the Wongsuwans immediately. Louise mentioned the telephone in the next room and he made the call. The officer came back presently and reported:

"The Wongsuwan family is very happy that you are not harmed. They want to show their appreciation for all that you have done by having you stay at their home for the rest of your visit."

"Perhaps we'll accept their kind invitation tomorrow," Aunt Harriet replied. "Right now the girls and I will go back to the Oriental Hotel and get a good night's sleep."

The next day the Danas were completely refreshed and ready to move out to the Wongsuwans' beautiful estate. Aunt Harriet had even lost her fear of lizards!

The Danas spent a delightful week relaxing and sightseeing. Pratoom's lovely face bloomed with happiness, now that she knew her husband was above suspicion, and Boonmi went out of his way to be hospitable to the Americans.

"In my stupidity I was swayed by my servant's story about you, but wanted proof myself, and I am afraid I treated you in a most unfriendly manner," he said. "I hope you will forgive me and accept these—"

Boonmi gave each of the Danas a beautiful scarf

and a matching purse. They thanked him, saying they thoroughly understood his position.

When the visitors announced they must return home, Jean said gaily to Malee, "We'll see you when Starhurst reopens."

"Yes," Malee replied, then laughed. "By that time, I imagine you two girls will have solved another mystery."

She was right. Louise and Jean, on their way home, became involved in another intriguing adventure, *The Sierra Gold Mystery*.

Before the Danas left Bangkok, the Wongsuwans presented them each with a beautiful ring set with star sapphires.

"And my golden Buddha statue has been returned to me," Malee told Louise and Jean as she was saying good-by to them at the airport. "The police found it in Mr. Holden's baggage. And my lovely bird is being sent to the school."

"How wonderful!" Louise said. "I always admired it, but now when I see the bamboo bird in your room, it will have a special significance. Fun, adventure—and, yes, danger!"